PRAISE FOR SARAH A. BAILEY

"*Heathen & Honeysuckle* is a second-chance masterpiece. **An absolute must-read.**"

- *USA Today* Bestselling Author Cali Melle

"*Wicked & Wildflower* is romance at its most breathtaking–emotion-packed and **brimming with delicious tension.** Sarah always creates a world you can get lost in, with characters so real it feels like they're sitting next to you, and *Wicked & Wildflower* is no exception. **Simply unputdownable.**"

- Bailey Hannah, author of *Alive & Wells*

"*Pacific Shores* is anything but fictional. It feels like a home away from home in the form of beautiful friendships, relatable characters, and **emotions that burst off the page**. This series is forever cemented in my soul."

- Emily Tudor, author of *The Road Not Taken*

"A perfect blend of **carefully crafted plot** and **irresistible heat.** Sarah is a master at creating relatable characters that you can't help but fall in love with...Her writing is both passionately sexy and **deeply heartfelt**, and *Wicked & Wildflower* is no exception. **Pure perfection.**"

- Ambar Cordova, author of the *Baker Oaks Series*

reckless
ROSES

reckless ROSES

SARAH A. BAILEY

PAGE & VINE

Page & Vine
An Imprint of Meredith Wild LLC

This is a work of fiction. Names, characters, places, and incidents either are the product of the author's imagination or are used fictitiously, and any resemblance to actual persons, living or dead, business establishments, events, or locales is entirely coincidental. The publisher does not assume any responsibility for third-party websites or their content.

The author acknowledges the trademarked status and trademark owners of various products referenced in this work, which have been used without permission. The publication/use of these trademarks is not authorized, associated with, or sponsored by the trademark owners.

Paperback ISBN: 978-1-964264-19-6

Author's Note

Dear Reader,

Welcome to Pacific Shores. If you've been here before, you may know what's to come as you begin *Reckless Roses*. If this is your first time visiting, please consider taking a look at the content warning below before you proceed.

While Pacific Shores is a romance series, *Reckless Roses* is the first book in a duet. The story continues in *Vice & Violet*.

Reckless Roses is intended for readers 18+ and contains sexually explicit material, as well as themes of grief and trauma that may be difficult for some. For a full list of content warnings, please visit my website: sarahabaileyauthor.com

With love,
S.A.B.

For those who love in secret and grieve in silence.

Chapter One

Elena

Age Twelve - January

"Jump Then Fall (Taylor's Version)" - Taylor Swift

"You're late, Miss Ramos," Mr. Holden, my seventh-grade algebra teacher, mutters as I interrupt the silence of his classroom, the slam of the metal door bouncing off the walls.

About thirty or so heads turn my way, and I force myself to glare. I'm not embarrassed. I didn't do anything wrong. *Stop staring.*

Lips sealed, I clear my throat and hand him my doctor's note. He slips a pair of glasses over his beady little eyes and reads through it at a glacial pace. Harrumphing, he hands it back to me and nods toward my seat at the back of the room. "We're working on textbook pages forty-six through fifty-two in partners. Whatever is not completed during class will be your homework for tonight." He sighs, looking around the room. "It appears everyone is already paired up." He waves his hand to his left, and I notice a tall, dark-haired boy sitting on the other side of Mr. Holden's desk, looking down at a book in his lap and not bothering to acknowledge my existence. "Zachary, can you please pair up with Elena for the remainder of the class period?"

The boy looks up, his brown eyes meeting mine. My stomach does a cartwheel, and I don't know why. I've never seen him before, but there are lots of boys I've never seen before, and they've never made my belly feel like a bird might fly out of my throat. His hair is almost black, flopping in the center of his forehead with a singular curl, and his gray T-shirt fits his arms perfectly. Speaking of *arms*, he has muscles. Biceps, in fact.

He stands, and *he's so tall.* Wow. His skin is perfectly smooth, a stark contrast from the pimply boils I'm coming face-to-face with every time a middle school boy gets a little too close to me. My eyes are drawn to his lips as he licks them. I've never noticed anyone's lips before, but I can't stop staring at his. I watch them turn into a smile until I can see his teeth, and now, my heart is beating about a million and a half miles per hour.

I shake my head, snapping out of whatever spell he has me under, realizing the class is still looking at me, Mr. Holden is still annoyed, I'm still not in my seat, and whoever this boy is, he's now waving at me. It's totally obvious I've been caught staring at him.

As fast as I can, I spin around and hustle to my desk, dropping my backpack on the ground with a *thunk* as I fall into my seat. The classroom slowly returns to the hum of a hundred different quiet conversations, but I only stare at my hands. Suddenly, I feel the presence of a person next to me, and before I can look at him, I'm being dragged sideways.

I snap my head up, and the boy—Zach—has a hand around the leg of my chair, pulling it closer to his. "Hi." He smiles.

"Hi," I murmur, careful not to show my teeth.

"You're Elena?"

I nod.

"I'm Zach. I'm Holden's T.A. this class period, so I can help you with your assignment."

I nod again, digging through my backpack for the textbook and my notebook. Red—because math is always red. I set it down on my desk, and Zach immediately pulls the textbook in front of him, flipping it open to the page we're supposed to be working on.

"So, do you speak, Elena? Or only make sound effects?"

I scoff.

"Guess that answers that question." There's a smile tugging at the corner of his mouth as his eyes remain on the page in front of him.

I let my curly hair fall against my face like a curtain to separate us. "I'm trying not to open my mouth today."

He laughs loudly, and my stomach does those cartwheels again, like making him laugh is something to be proud of.

"Why?"

"I got braces."

He turns to face me, and his stare heats my cheeks. He doesn't speak until I look at him. "Do your teeth hurt?"

I shrug. Dropping my head again, I say, "I mostly just don't want anyone to see them. They're ugly."

"Why don't you let me be the judge of that?" His voice is so smooth; it sounds like butter, if butter made noise when it glided against toast. I don't like the way I can feel it. Or maybe I do like it, and that freaks me out. That's the part I don't like.

No way am I showing him my braces. Heat creeps up my neck, and it must show in my cheeks because he laughs again.

"C'mon. I'm joking." He bumps his shoulder against mine, and those cartwheels start spinning faster, in a way that makes it hard to catch my breath.

"Why have I never seen you before?" I ask.

His smile grows wider, and again, I can't stop staring at how soft his skin looks. His cheeks are a natural rosy color, but I like it. I kind of want to touch them. He has big, broad shoulders, and veins in his arms that run into his clenched fists atop the desk.

I think he has definitely gone through puberty already. Even my brother hasn't gone through puberty. His voice still cracks, and he only has, like, three armpit hairs. Zach's is deep. I bet Zach grows hair all over the place.

My cheeks heat. *God, why am I thinking about his body hair*?

"I'm in eighth grade." He shrugs. "And my family just moved to town this past summer."

That explains it. We don't share any classes with eighth graders, not unless they're a teacher's assistant, I guess. "Oh."

His arm touches mine again, and it feels like a bird's wings are flapping in my chest. "I still think you're cute when you're talking, by the way."

"You think I'm cute?" I blurt.

He tilts his head, smirking. "Don't pretend like you don't know you're cute, Elena. I'm sure boys tell you that all the time."

I shrug. Yeah, boys have had crushes on me before, at least, I think. "Most boys are too afraid to talk to me. They only want to text, and I share a phone with my brother." I roll my eyes. "And he's crazy."

Zach laughs. "Well, they're missing out, because you're pretty when you blush."

"Thanks," I murmur, hiding my face.

Is he flirting with me? He must be flirting with me.

Why does my whole body feel hot? Why do I feel like I'm going to throw up?

"Bet you're even prettier when you smile." He mindlessly twists his finger in one of the curls hanging by my shoulder. He's so close to touching me, but he's not, and I kind of wish he were.

I've had boys pass me notes in class, or had their friends

run up to me at lunchtime to tell me someone has a crush on me. I've had boys ask for my phone number and then ask me to date them over text message, but I've never had a boy tell me I'm pretty right to my face.

I don't think anyone has ever had the courage before.

Zach thinks I'm pretty, and he's touching my hair. He's smiling at me, and *he* wants *me* to smile at him too. That makes me feel like I have wings, like my stomach is flying out of my chest and doing somersaults down the street.

I thought I'd had crushes on boys before—boys I thought were cute, or maybe funny.

But this feeling of flying is something new, something I think I hate because it's scary, but at the same time, I don't want it to go away.

I realize I'm frowning.

As quickly as possible, I flash him a smile, hoping he can't see the brackets on my teeth, and then I return to my resting frown-face.

He chuckles. "Yeah, you're pretty when you smile."

"Even with the braces?"

"Definitely."

I can't help the small giggle that comes out of my mouth. I *never* giggle. He tugs on the hair wrapped around his finger, opening his mouth to say something just as the bell rings, signaling the end of the class period.

His mouth clamps shut, and he slides my textbook back to me. "We didn't get much work done." Snatching my pen from my hand, he grabs my notebook and scribbles something down. "Here's my number. I get home from practice around seven." He stands from the table, smirking down at me. "And you can call me. That way, your crazy brother won't see our texts."

Words, thoughts, and my entire stomach are caught inside

my throat.

I'm basically a blushing, giggling, gaping fish at this point. Embarrassing.

He doesn't wait for me to respond. He walks to the front and swipes his backpack from the floor, tossing it over his shoulder. I'm paying way too much attention to the way he looks in a pair of jeans. As if he knows it too, he turns back one more time, winking at me before he exits the classroom.

My face feels like it's covered in flames, my heart beating out of my chest, and I spend the rest of the day counting down the seconds until I can call him and ask him to help me with my homework, even though homework is the last thing on my mind.

Chapter Two

August

Age Eleven - May

"Hey Girl" - Stephen Sanchez

Late May sunshine burns the back of my head as I climb to the top of Hillside Road, making my way home from school. Adjusting to life in Pacific Shores hasn't been the most pleasant experience, and I couldn't be more excited that the school year is about to end.

Moving to a new town, a new school, and a new grade as the runt kid isn't fun for anyone, I'm sure. Today was extra rough, though. I get teased for still wearing glasses because I'm afraid of contact lenses, or for spending lunch hour reading a book rather than playing kickball. But the worst part is, *I don't care* if other kids make fun of me for it, and that seems to upset them more. So, they get meaner, harsher, more aggressive.

As I reach the end of our road, the big, purple trees that line our yard are on full display. I think my mom calls them jacarandas or something. They were regular old green trees when we moved into the house last summer, but earlier this spring, they exploded into bright purple flowers, covering our entire lawn in shades of violet and lavender.

What I don't expect as I close in on my parents' two-story house is a girl. She has to be around the same age as me, long, dark hair falling down her back as she hoists herself onto a higher branch of the jacaranda tree, holding her T-shirt out in front of her and plucking flowers off the stems, letting them fall into the pouch her shirt creates.

I step closer to her, standing on the sidewalk and watching from below as she climbs higher and higher. She doesn't seem to notice me, which gives me a second to study her closely. She's small, like me, wearing a black shirt and a pair of jeans, that dark curly hair swept back into a low ponytail that sways between her shoulders as she concentrates on picking a flower above her head.

"Hey!" I call out.

She gasps, head snapping down at my voice. She stumbles, rocking sideways and nearly losing her balance. My stomach shrinks up, afraid she'll fall, before she catches herself on the branch she's sitting on. Unfortunately, all the flowers in her shirt spill, sprinkling to the ground in front of me like snowflakes.

"Dammit!" she shrieks.

I run up to the tree, gathering her fallen petals in my own shirt. "Sorry," I hiss. "I didn't mean to scare you."

"Well, what did you think was gonna happen?" she mutters as she effortlessly shimmies down the trunk, jumping to the ground right in front of me.

I finish picking up her flowers, gathering them in my shirt like she did, but when I straighten and see her face up close for the first time, the fabric falls from my grasp and her flowers tumble to the ground again.

She's the prettiest girl I've ever seen.

With her hands on her hips, her brown eyes are narrowed to slits as she glares at me, but at just the right angle, the sun shines on them, and they look like caramel syrup. Her lips are turned into a frown, and for the first time in my life, I find myself wanting to say or do something—anything—to make a girl smile.

Those eyes slowly drag from my face to my feet, watching her flowers pile on the grass for the second time. She crosses her arms, sighing, before lifting her gaze.

"What are you staring at?"

That snaps me out of it. I squat all too quickly. "No—nothing." I begin gathering her flowers again.

She drops to her knees in front of me, helping pick up the petals. "Who are you?"

"My name is Augustus," I say, unsure why my voice is shaking. "But most people call me August. I guess the effort of those last two letters is too much for them."

She laughs at that, and my chest feels like it's going to explode.

"My name is Elena, but my friend Leo calls me Lena. I guess the E is too much work for him, too." I match her laughter, and she raises her eyes to my face with a smirk. "So, why are you yelling at girls in trees, Augustus?"

I shrug. "I was just wondering what you were doing in my front yard."

Her eyes go wide, and if I'm not mistaken, a bit of a blush colors her cheeks. "This is your house?"

I laugh again, nodding.

"My whole life, I only knew Miss Waterson to live here, and I thought she was way too old to have a kid."

"Was that the lady who lived here before us?" I chuckle. "I think they moved her into a home. My parents bought the house last summer."

"Oh." She looks at her hands, seeming embarrassed. "Miss Waterson was so old, she never noticed when I'd steal her flowers in the spring. I guess I'll have to stop doing that, then."

"My mom definitely wouldn't like you climbing our tree,

but...I could? If you wanted. I'll pick the flowers for you."

A smile explodes on her cheeks, but she hides it just as quickly. "You don't have to do that."

"I don't mind!" I find myself shouting, and her head rears back, as if surprised by my eagerness. *Rein it in, Augustus.* I'm bad at talking to girls in general, even the ones who don't make my stomach hurt with how pretty they are, and Elena is by far the prettiest. "I mean..." I clear my throat. "It's no big deal. Do you live far?"

She hides a knowing smile, and I feel stupid. "No. Just one street over. Oceanside Avenue."

"Are you in middle school?" I ask. "I feel like I would've noticed you if we went to school together, so you must be older." She smiles at me again, and I notice the purple and black chains across her teeth. "I like the color of your braces. Is purple your favorite color?"

Jesus, why am I asking her so many questions?

Somebody tape my mouth shut.

She snorts. "Yes, I'm in middle school. I'm in seventh grade." Elena smiles to herself, plucking at the petals of the small flower in her hand. "And yeah, purple is my favorite color. Wild violets are my favorite flowers. I love that they're all purple and then have a little burst of yellow in the middle." She shrugs. "My dad calls them weeds, but I think they're pretty. I like to let them dry out and make bookmarks out of them. But I add other flowers too, and since these trees don't bloom all year round, I try to pick some before they die," she says, waving to the drooping bundles of purple flowers above our heads.

"I like purple too," I respond. "And I like to read."

Her head snaps up, and the most genuine smile I think I've ever seen flashes across her face. "Really? What's your favorite book?"

"Right now? Probably Percy Jackson and the Olympians."

Elena shoots up on her knees, crossing the space between us and setting a hand on my knee. Every atom in my body seems to head straight for her touch, and I'm buzzing. "I *love* Percy Jackson!" She's the one squealing with excitement now, and I can't help the smile it brings to my face. "I annotated the whole series!"

"What's annotating?" I ask, trying to think of anything other than the way her hand feels on my leg.

"Oh, it's like...highlighting your favorite passages and making little notes in the margins, putting tabs on those pages so you can go back and find them later." She smiles at me. "Sometimes, I draw little doodles too, but I'm not very good at drawing. I don't like doing things I'm no good at."

That makes me laugh for some reason. "I like to draw."

Her head tilts sideways, and I decide her smile is my favorite one I've ever seen. "Are you good at it? Drawing?"

I shrug. "My mom says I am."

She's laughing at me now. Her head drops, and for the first time, I think she realizes she's touching me. She quickly removes her hand and falls back onto the grass. "I like you, Augustus."

Is this what having a heart attack feels like?

My heart is beating so hard, I wonder if it's leaving an imprint beneath my shirt. I can't breathe because my stomach is blocking my airway, but somehow, I say the words, "I like you too, Elena."

She smiles to herself, stuffing the flower petals into her shirt as she stands. "Do you want to hang out this weekend? I can bring you my copy of *The Lightning Thief* so you can see my annotations?"

I try to keep myself calm, but the truth is, I want to scream and run in circles like an excited puppy. "Sure." I force myself to stay on the ground, to stop my smile from growing too wide. "That sounds fun."

"Have you been to Sweet Rue's on the Boardwalk? We could meet there and get ice cream?"

"Okay." I'm lactose intolerant, but I'm not about to tell her that. I'll eat all the ice cream and suffer everything that comes afterward if I get to see her again.

I get up and swipe the dirt from my knees. "I'm normally not allowed to go down to the Boardwalk without my older brother, Zach, but he won't care. He'll just leave me at the ice cream shop and go surfing or something."

Elena's entire body goes still. Where she was vibrating with excitement before, she's frozen now. "Zach?" she asks, tilting her head. "Wait, what's your last name?"

"Hayes," I say. "My brother is in eighth grade, so you go to school with him. I'm only in sixth grade."

Her jaw drops, pretty brown eyes going wide with shock. "Your brother is *Zach Hayes*?"

"Yeah?"

"Oh shit." Elena steps back, planting herself on the sidewalk in front of the house. "Zach Hayes lives *here*? I was climbing Zach Hayes's *tree*?"

"I guess?"

I'm confused. That is, until I notice her breathing increase, notice the change in color on her cheeks, the way she frantically looks around my home, gazing through its windows as if she's searching for something. Someone.

It hits me then.

"You know my brother?"

It's the way she drops her head, hides her smile, and tucks a strand of hair behind her ear. I've seen way too many girls do that way too many times in Zach's presence.

"Yeah." She bites her lip, blushing. "I mean...we talk on the phone sometimes. He helps me with my math homework."

The butterflies begging to explode out of my body only moments ago all seem to perish, their still wings like dead weight inside the bottom of my stomach. Disappointment punches me right in the gut, making me fight the urge to keel over and die right along with those butterflies.

Elena is the prettiest girl I've ever seen.

She likes my favorite book. She didn't call me a loser when I told her I draw.

She's funny. She told me she liked me. When I made her smile, I felt something in my chest I've never felt before.

And Elena has a crush on my older brother.

She's still looking toward the front of my house, the massive purple tree hanging over us like a daydream, the house behind it acting as the harsh, unfair reality that is my brother. He's handsome—with perfect eyesight—and charming. He plays just about every sport ever invented, and he's the captain of every team. He has gone through puberty and had his growth spurt while I'm still small. He always says the right thing, knows how to talk to girls. I'm awkward and shy.

I hate him sometimes. I hate him most of all right now.

"He's not home right now," I say to Elena, trying to keep my voice still. "He doesn't get home until after—"

"Baseball practice." She nods. "Yeah, I know. I must've forgotten." Her eyes meet mine, and suddenly, all that intense focus has fallen back on me. Suddenly, I don't care about my brother. I don't care about much of anything except her looking at me. "So...Sweet Rue's on Saturday at noon?"

She still wants to hang out with me?

Speechless, I only nod.

Elena smiles again, and it's not the meek, hidden blush that appeared when I mentioned my brother. It's bigger, it's real. Something she's not afraid to hide from me, though I wonder if her smile is something she tries to hide from others.

"If you can't come, just have your brother text me and let me know." She begins down the sidewalk toward Oceanside Avenue. "Bye, Augustus!" She waves before she's out of sight.

"Bye, Elena." I wave back.

I still feel the burn of her touch on my knee as I stare down at the sprinkles of purple flowers she left behind. I pick them up, gathering them in my pockets before I go inside.

I know I had a horrible day before I stumbled upon her, but now, I can't seem to remember what was so bad.

Chapter Three

August

Age Thirteen - June

"Please Don't Be" - Hazlett

"Wake up, Augustus," a soft voice sings from somewhere outside my head.

In my mind, I'm dreaming of that voice too.

A sting races through the underside of my arm. My eyes fly open, and I shoot upright in bed, slapping away whatever the hell just bit me. As I check my arms for signs of some insect, her laughter filters through my ears, and suddenly, my body is on alert for an entirely different reason. I hike my comforter up my chest, ensuring it's not so tight that she can see exactly what's going on beneath it.

Turning sideways, I find Elena on her knees at the edge of my bed, smiling at me.

"What are you doing?" I ask, wiping my eyes.

"It's time." Her grin is mischievous, the same expression her twin makes at me when he's trying to get me to break the law. It's fucking terrifying on both of them.

"Time for what?"

Another burst of laughter comes from farther away, and for the first time this morning, I take in my surroundings. My bedroom door is thrown wide open and my two best friends are standing in the doorway, giving me the same fucked-up smile as Elena.

Her twin brother, Everett, leans against my door with his arms crossed. He has grown at least six inches in the last year, and now, he towers above all of us, including Zach. I again tug my blankets farther up my body, somehow feeling like he can see right through my face and into my dreams.

Leo stands next to him, painfully resembling that kid from *High School Musical*. His blue eyes glisten with knowing, and the smile he gives me is different from the twins'.

"Get up, buttercup." Elena pats my cheek a few times, stealing my attention the way she always does. "We're going pier jumping."

I roll my eyes, lying back against my headboard. "I told you guys I didn't want to do that."

I'm not as reckless as my friends. I just don't see the point in it, I guess. Everett's got a wild nature that calls him to try everything just for the thrill. Leo does stupid shit because he wants attention. He was neglected and abandoned, so that tracks. My brother wants to be the cool, older leader the others look up to, and Elena... I think Elena has always been a little insecure about her inability to click with other girls, and the only way to keep up with the boys is to be as crazy as they are. I know there are parts of her that enjoy it, being untamed. She was destined for it, but not through the actions she takes to fit in with the boys. It's Elena's heart that's wild, and ironically, that's the part of her she keeps locked in a cage.

Her dark lashes flutter as she bats her eyes at me, sticking out her bottom lip. She thinks she's dramatically pouting, but what she doesn't know is that the pleading look on her face makes me want to give her anything she has ever asked for. Sometimes, I'm afraid if she knew the effect she had on me, she'd take advantage of it. "Please, Augustus. I'm *daring* you."

Yeah, see, that word means nothing to me. Leo and Everett—even my brother—can't turn down dares easily. The three of them are constantly playing a game of chicken at school and around town, daring each other to do something stupid, like blind skateboarding down a steep hill in traffic, or go shopping cart surfing, or spray paint over the street sign for Pacific Tides Blvd so it says "Pacific Tits Blvd" instead.

Idiots.

Jumping off the pier together is one of the tamer hobbies our group has taken up over the last several weeks. It started when Everett dared Leo to jump off one morning. Leaping from the Pacific Shores pier is against the law, and there is a thousand-dollar fine if you're caught—plus, you get permanently banned from the Boardwalk.

Leo did it anyway, and the week after, he dared Everett, who dared Zach the week after that, and Zach dared Elena last week. Now, apparently, it's my turn. Even though I don't care much for this kind of stuff, being chosen last is never fun, which made me want to participate even less.

I'm hellbent on saying no; I won't let myself be the lame younger friend who tags along out of pity. I huff, crossing my arms and facing Elena again. She's still giving me that hopeful expression, and as her lip quivers and her head tilts, I notice her hair fall off one shoulder and behind her back. The thin, black strap of a swimsuit peeks out from the shoulder of her tank top, and I know *exactly* what suit she's wearing. It's the one she had last summer. That bathing suit is made up of exactly two tiny triangles that leave very little to the imagination, with thin bottoms that are no better.

Dammit.

My eyes trail down the column of her neck to her chest, imagining what she looks like without that tank top on—the way she'll look when she's peeling her shorts off at the pier, when she climbs up on the railing, when she jumps off the edge. "Fine. I'll go."

That mischievous grin flashes across her mouth as she softly claps her hands together, and I realize the only thing that may be more motivating to me than her body is her smile.

"August, if you're coming, you need to get your ass out of bed! Let's go!" Zach booms from the front of our house—likely the kitchen.

Elena winks as she backs off my bed at Zach's voice. She always seems to be chasing after him in one way or another—that much hasn't changed over the course of the last year. I knew the day I met her, she must've had a crush on him, but with the way he has consistently treated her, I hoped it'd dissipate with time.

Seventh grade was good—with Zach in high school and me in middle school, I was finally in the same place as Elena. I had seven hours each day I was guaranteed not to lose her attention to him. We didn't have any of the same classes, since she's a year older, but we ate lunch together most days, and we read together in the library during study hall. We spent months trading books we annotated for each other.

Even this past year after Elena transitioned into high school for ninth grade, we remained just as close.

Some weekends, we meet up at Sweet Rue's or at my house, and I draw while she writes in her journal. She doesn't tell me what she's writing, but she seems to love it as much as I love my sketchbook. We read together, we like the same music and the same movies. My stomach still hurts every time I make her laugh, and she listens to what I say like it's the most interesting thing she has ever heard. She makes me feel important, and she never makes me feel forgotten.

Leo and Everett spend just about every free minute they have on the water, and when Zach isn't at football, baseball, or basketball practice, he's doing the same. I like surfing, and I'm okay at it, but I'm nothing compared to Leo. Some people call him a prodigy, and I can't keep up with him and Everett. Elena likes the slower pace surfing like I do, the kind that's not competitive or intense, but simple and peaceful. Sometimes, all we do is paddle beyond the break and float, lying on our backs as we look up at the sky and make shapes out of clouds.

Those days are my most favorite of all.

Some days, I'm convinced Elena was put on this planet just for me. Sometimes, I'm convinced she's my other half. My soulmate, maybe. Without question, I know she's my best friend in the world, but there is part of me that does question—that wants—so much more.

And yet, I watch in silence as she closes my bedroom door behind her, off in search of my brother.

A half hour later, the five of us are standing above the railing, staring down into the morphing shades of blue that make up the Pacific. The water is nearly crystalline in the morning sun, glowing out across the white caps from behind us, casting the crashing waves in sparkles. The reflection leaps across the ever-moving water, making it a thousand different colors all at once. My stomach jumps a little, realizing how far the drop actually is.

"Okay, Auggie, you've got to go first because it's your dare, and the rest of us will follow," Leo shouts from the other end, Everett, Zach, and Elena between us.

"Oh, fuck you," I scoff. "I'm not jumping alone so you can all laugh at me and then run away." They'd totally do something like that, and they know it.

"Fine, fucker." Everett turns around, nearly slipping off the rail as he puts his back to the ocean. He looks at me with a shit-eating grin and his middle finger in the air as he leaps backward, dropping into the water below.

We all watch him disappear beneath the surface, and there is an innate kind of fear that overcomes you when you watch someone get swallowed up by waves. The air held captive inside my lungs is let go when Everett's head bursts from the water only a second later.

"Let's fucking go!" he shouts as he treads below us.

Elena's hand darts out to grab mine. "Ready?"

Sparks alight across my skin where she touches me, fire spreading through every inch as I soak in the view of her next to me. She winks, and I know exactly what she's doing. She can tell I'm not comfortable with this, and she's making sure I know I'm safe.

She'd never call me out in front of my friends, and she'd never judge me for being less courageous than the rest of them, but she'll hold my hand while she encourages me to be wild all the same.

Another moment cementing my belief that we might be soulmates.

I nod, watching her feet leave the railing a fraction of a second before I leap along with her. Time flashes as we fall through the air, and suddenly, I'm engulfed in the shocking cold of the ocean. Our bodies sink down between the waves, and my eyes are screwed shut, but I can feel her next to me. Her hand grips mine, our legs brushing as we kick toward the surface. The *whoosh* of water rushes past my ears as she strokes our arms, pushing us upward.

The sun's rays greet my skin as I break through the water, opening my eyes and blinking at the daylight. My blurry vision mostly clears, though I can't see perfectly without my glasses. Still, I do make out Leo and Everett racing through the waves toward the shore. Elena pulls her hand from mine, laughing as she wipes wet hair from her eyes. Zach treads water nearby, watching us intensely—as if trying to see whether our limbs were entwined beneath the surface. If I'm not mistaken, there may be jealousy on his face, and my chest swells with some kind of strange pride at the sight.

As Zach's eyes meet mine, that expression is wiped away by a smile. He cuts through the water, closing the distance between us. Lifting himself up, he places two hands on top of my head and tries pushing me below again. "Look at you, baby bro. You did it."

"Fuck off," I gargle through a mouth of salt water as he pushes me down.

I grab his arms and shove him off me, but he only laughs, finally letting me go in a show of strength and mercy.

Zach is athletic, while I am...not as much. I have endurance, sure. I've always been fast and agile, but sports just don't interest me. It makes sense that we have different builds and tastes and interests, given that Zach is adopted. My mother was supposedly unable to get pregnant not long after my parents got married, so they went through the process of adopting Zach. A year or so later, she miraculously got pregnant with me.

People don't comment on it much; it's not noticeable enough to most. He has dark features and light skin like my dad. They don't necessarily look alike, but it's not enough for most to question a relation. I am, however, the spitting image of my mother—or so I'm told.

She was born in Greece and moved to the United States after being discovered by a modeling agency while on a trip to Amsterdam as a teen. She was a fairly prominent soap opera star in the nineties and has often been dubbed one of the most beautiful women in the world, so I can't complain. I've got her forest-green eyes, olive-toned skin, and a sprinkle of freckles that's most visible in the summer, plus her chestnut brown curls.

Being the miracle baby-twin to our mother is something that has always bothered Zach. He doesn't say it out loud, but we can all see it. He does a decent job of not taking it out on me, at least.

I'm pulled from my thoughts as I realize both Zach and Elena are at least fifteen yards ahead of me now, paddling toward shore. Leo and Everett are already back on land, discarding the waterproof backpack Leo jumped with as they put on their clothes. By the time Elena and Zach reach the beach, Leo and Everett are long gone—likely off to meet some girls from school at Sweet Rue's, like they mentioned earlier.

The water finally becomes shallow enough for me to plant my feet in the sand, and I dunk my head one more time to smooth back my hair. As I come back up, I find my brother and my best friend standing on the shore, far closer than I'd like. He's holding her arm just above the elbow, rubbing his thumb across her skin. She's smiling up at him like he hung the goddamn moon, laughing as he whispers something in her ear.

Elena's mouth moves, and whatever my brother responds with makes her bite her lip and blush in the way I've been so desperate to make her do, but have never accomplished. Zach raises his arm, gripping her chin and extending his thumb to pull her bottom lip from her teeth. Elena nods, looking at him in a way she has never looked at me.

And my chest caves in, heart begging me to wash away with the tide as I watch my brother kiss the girl of my dreams.

Elena

"Should we wait for August?" I ask, paddling after Zach as he swims to shore.

He turns around, wading backward. "He's fine. He's right behind us." Flashing me the familiar grin that makes my stomach flip, he adds, "I wanted a minute alone with you anyway."

That flip becomes a lurch, hurling out of my throat as I choke on air. I stumble over my own breath in the most embarrassing way possible. Zach doesn't seem surprised, probably because I always act like a fucking idiot around him.

Alone with me?

The question ping-pongs inside my skull as we make our way to the shore. Climbing out of the water puts my whole body on alert, suddenly extremely aware of what I'm wearing and how I look. Salt water doesn't do much for my curly hair, which I'm sure is resembling some kind of rat's nest. I brush it behind my shoulder before smoothing a hand over the top of my head. Zach smirks as he watches me, reaching out to tug at the strap of my swimsuit.

"I like this on you."

"Thanks," I murmur. I can never muster the words to respond when he compliments me. It feels like a privilege to have his attention on my body, and a measly *thanks* doesn't seem enough to express the feeling that manifests inside my bones at his praise.

But telling him *that* would be crazy.

"How did you like jumping off the pier the second time?"

I shrug. "Felt the same as the first, I guess? Fun. The boys are annoying."

His brows furrow. "Me?"

"Never." I shake my head, hiding a laugh.

That's true. Zach, despite being only a year older, is far more mature than Leo and Everett. I don't know if it's because the two of them are my brothers—Leo not technically, but since he moved in with us and my parents have become his legal guardians, it seems like the more fitting title—and therefore destined to bother me, or if it's because there is something special about Zach himself.

Zach and I don't have much in common, not the way August and I do. He doesn't read for fun, and I don't play sports. He's popular, and I hate the general population most days. But every time I speak to him about books, he understands exactly what I'm saying. Every time I have an irrationally bad day, he reminds me that there are far worse things to be upset about in life than mean girls at school or accidentally finding my twin brother's nude photos on our shared computer. He doesn't treat me like a child, and he doesn't allow me to act like one either.

He makes me feel older, and that makes me think harder.

Plus, he's... My eyes trail down the length of his bare torso. He's broad, toned, covered in muscle. He looks like an athlete, and I never thought I'd care much about that, but...well, his body definitely makes my heartbeat low in my stomach, so it's doing something for me.

"Elena," he rasps, snapping me out of my stare-down with his pecs. "I asked you a question."

"What?" I realize he's still holding the strap of my bathing suit.

"I asked you to describe what it felt like to jump off that pier using one of your big-girl-book words." His hand runs down the length of my arm, leaving goosebumps in its wake.

I roll my eyes. Zach doesn't read, but he at least has the

basic understanding that reading expands one's vocabulary. Every time he comes over, or we meet up on the beach, he asks me to tell him a word I read that day. I'm always searching for the craziest, most astounding words to impress him with, mostly because I like the way it feels when I make him laugh.

It doesn't take long to find a word fitting of the way this moment feels.

"Exhilarating," I breathe.

"Hmm." He smiles, stepping into me. Suddenly, the beach and the pier and everything around me disappears. All I see is him. Smooth skin, dark eyes, full lips. "I'll bet I can give you a much better use of that one."

"How?" My voice is hardly a whisper, no doubt drowned out by the sound of crashing waves, but somehow, he hears me anyway.

"Have you ever been kissed, Elena?"

I shake my head.

"Do you want to be?"

I nod, glad he's not asking me for a word right now, because they don't exist to me.

I've been watching Zach Hayes for over a year now. I've been trying my damnedest to garner his attention and make him laugh. I've seen his hands and felt his skin in my daydreams—the ones I have when I close my eyes at night, too. I always wonder if he watches back, if he could be thinking the same thing. It feels impossible because he's older, smarter, more popular than me.

And yet...he's asking to kiss me.

Wings flap inside my chest as his hand hooks around the nape of my neck, twisting in my hair. He tilts my head upward, and suddenly, his drops down. I let my eyes fall closed, and I don't just feel my heartbeat in my stomach—I feel it in every cell of my body. My head is swimming; my feet don't feel like they're on the ground, but in the clouds.

Electrifying. Burning. Thrilling. *Exhilarating.*

Words float through my mind as Zach presses his lips to mine, and I wonder if these are the words to describe what falling in love feels like.

Chapter Four

Elena

Age Fifteen - May

"Video Games" - *Lana Del Rey*

"Augustus, you're not being helpful."

I spin in my desk chair, looking up at my best friend. His dark brown curls flop against his forehead, as per usual. Brows are furrowed beneath his black-rimmed glasses, and he scratches his chin, the faintest stubble scratching against his fingertips.

"I don't know what to tell you, Elena. You'll look beautiful in anything."

"Lies. You're a dirty little liar."

His deep-green eyes flick from the computer to my face, crinkling with amusement. "Okay, I can't picture you in tulle, glitter, or the color orange, but anything else would be perfect."

I *despise* the color orange.

"I think I want to wear red." I click through the seventeen tabs on my computer screen again, each one featuring a different style of prom dress. I'm losing my mind.

"You hate red."

"It's Zach's favorite color." I swallow, refusing to make eye contact. "And he asked me, so...you know..."

Zach is so damn wishy-washy with me. Around my brothers and at school, he pretends I'm no more than the sister of his best friends. Then, he calls me late at night and we talk into the early hours of the morning about everything in life. He tells me I'm his favorite person. Some weekends, he sneaks into my bedroom in the middle of the night, and we cuddle. We've kissed often behind closed doors and under the veil of darkness. He tells me I'm beautiful. He tells me he has fallen for me.

But when light shines, it's like I've made it all up.

I see him flirt with girls at school—ones he insists are just friends. I hear rumors of him hooking up with people at parties, and he tells me they're all lies. I ask him why he doesn't want to call me his girlfriend, why he won't kiss me or hold my hand out in the open; he insists it's because it would make things weird with my brothers, that he doesn't want to affect the dynamic of our friendships. He doesn't want to *complicate* things.

I convince myself he's embarrassed to be with me, but he tells me that's not true, that I'm overreacting. The wheel spins round and round, the way it has the past few years.

But last week, he finally asked me to be his prom date. The rest of us are too young to attend, since prom is reserved for the junior and senior classes only—unless you're invited as the date of an upperclassman. Everett was asked to prom by some twelfth-grade girl he's sleeping with, and I was invited by Zach. Leo and August don't get to go, but they don't seem to care either way.

It feels like a coming out of sorts for Zach and me. He can't pretend there's nothing between us if he's taking me to prom. He can't hide it from my brother either. There is no excuse to continue keeping us in the dark, and I'm hopeful by the end of this weekend, I'll officially have the coveted label of Zach Hayes' Girlfriend.

"Just because he asked you to prom doesn't mean you need

to conform to what he wants. You should wear a dress—and a color—you feel best in."

"I mean," I shrug, "Zach thinks I look good in red. He said that every time I wore Everett's football jersey to a game last fall." Our school colors are red, black, and silver. More than a few fights had broken out between my brother's various *flings*, so he told all the girls he'd been seeing at the time that I had asked to wear his jersey to every game that season.

I didn't give a fuck about what I wore to a high school football game or who had my twin's number on their back, but he did agree to do my laundry for the entire first semester of the school year, so it was worth it.

"He's not wrong," August relents, crossing my room and flopping down onto my bed. He pulls his sketchbook out of his backpack and starts shading the piece he's been working on for a while. He won't show me what it is until it's finished, though.

"We weren't done," I grumble. "I need to choose which dress."

"The silky, strapless, formfitting one," he says without looking up. I quickly click through my laundry list of options until I find the one I'm sure he's referring to. "Your boobs will look great in that."

"Augustus!" I spin to face him, my cheeks warming.

He glances up at me, utmost seriousness on his face, with zero embarrassment. "What? You wanted me to be honest—that's me being honest."

I snort, rolling my eyes as I throw a pencil across my room and hit him in the chest. He only smiles, placing it between his teeth as he looks back down at whatever he's drawing.

"I don't know what you want me to tell you, Elena."

"I want you to tell me that I didn't buy a brand-new dress and spend hours on my hair and makeup only for you to bail on me the day of!" My voice cracks on the last word, hot, angry tears streaming down my face.

"Please tell me you're not crying." He doesn't say it like he cares. No, he says it like he's *annoyed*. "You're being overdramatic. You have two more years to attend prom. You can just wear the dress then."

"It's not about that!" My words tremble. "You *promised* me. You asked me to be *your* date." I suck in a sharp breath, shaking with emotion and feeling like I'm overreacting but unable to stop it. "You got my hopes up, Zach."

That shuts him up, silence on the other end of my phone. Finally, he sighs. "I'm sorry, baby. You know I'd never mean to hurt you."

I don't know that, actually. He seems to not think much before he acts, and his actions have hurt me more than a few times.

"Kelsey's boyfriend broke up with her yesterday. She was going to skip prom entirely, and it's her last year to attend. She's just a friend, but...I hated the idea of her losing out on this experience because she decided to date a douchebag."

My only response is a tearful hiccup.

"We're just going as friends, I swear. We're attending with a large group of the guys on the baseball team and their dates. I won't even slow dance with her. I'll leave right after the dance, and I'll come see you, okay?"

I don't bother responding to that. I only ask, "Why couldn't someone else take her? Why'd you have to volunteer?"

"Well, all the other guys are taking their girlfriends. I am the only one who doesn't—"

"Good night, Zach. Please don't come over after the dance."

I hang up before he has the chance to finish his sentence or attempt to convince me I'm overthinking things. He said exactly what I needed to hear: he very much *does not* see me as girlfriend material.

I drop my phone onto my bed, turning to face the full-body mirror hanging on the back of my door. August was right; this dress makes my tits look amazing. It's tight enough at the bust that they swell above the neckline, and satin sweeps across my waist, gathering on the left side, accentuating my minimal curves. A high slit at my upper thigh shows off my skin and my strappy black heels, while the other side of the dress freely flows to the floor like liquid.

I kind of wish it were purple. An amethyst tone would be beautiful, but even in red, I look phenomenal.

Fuck Zach Hayes.

As my eyes raise to my face, I notice my eyeliner running down my cheeks, ruining the carefully crafted makeup I worked so hard on, and then I remember, it doesn't matter anyway. I was stood up. My first and only school dance, I was stood up by my date. Not just my date, but the boy I've been in love with since the age of twelve.

My hands clench as I fight the urge to start throwing shit. Instead, I stomp over to my bed and fall back onto it. Sending a text to my mother, I let her know I won't be attending prom and not to come into my room until I emerge. After a few meltdowns around the age of thirteen, Mom and I came to an understanding that I need to rage alone, and when I'm ready to talk, I'll make it known. She has done a good job of giving me space when I need it ever since.

Thankfully, Everett already left to pick up his date, and Leo is with August down at the boardwalk today. I won't have to face my brothers tonight, but Zach will have to face Everett at the dance, and part of me kind of hopes Everett hits him for bailing on me.

As I settle into bed, still clad in my dress and shoes, my tears come in a free fall, soaking me in rejection. I pull my poetry book from my bedside table and begin scribbling down my emotions. If nothing else, I can create art with my pain.

Exhaustion stings my eyes as I squint at the book in my lap. I swore I was only going to read a few chapters and then I'd finally change out of my prom dress, accept the night for the bust it was, and go to bed.

Except, it has been four hours since I started reading, I'm nearly seventy percent through, and the enemies just kissed for the first time.

I'm dead set on finishing the book before I let myself fall asleep—until I hear a knock against my bedroom window, followed by the chime of my phone.

I check my phone first, seeing a text message from August:

Don't freak out. It's me.

I scramble from under my comforter and lean over the foot of my bed, where it rests near my window. Reaching as far as I can, I draw my blinds and throw the window open. I can just make out his silhouette a few feet away.

"What are you doing?" I ask.

"I heard your night didn't go well." I can't really see him, but his voice is clear as day, and it feels like comfort. "I wanted to check in on you."

"I'm okay." I shrug as I move off my bed, leaning my upper

body out my window.

"You're still wearing your dress."

I glance down at my chest, realizing I am still, in fact, wearing my dress. "Well, my tits look great, so..."

He laughs, stepping up to the window so I can see his face more clearly. August is handsome in a magical kind of way. His features don't look like they belong to real people, like they should instead be reserved for celebrities and models we can convince ourselves don't actually exist.

His boyish smile shines even in the dark, emerald eyes sparkling behind his glasses. "Do you want to go somewhere? Get out of the house for a bit?"

I was tired a few moments ago, but fresh air against my cheeks and the sound of my best friend's voice hits like a shot of espresso. I'm wired and ready to go anywhere with him.

"Sure, let's go." I pull back inside my room, running to my closet to swap my heels for Converse before sneaking back over to my window and reaching my hand out for August to grab.

"You don't want to change first?" he asks.

"Someone should see me in this dress, Augustus."

He chuckles. "Glad it's me."

I smile as he pulls me through the window, and I straddle one leg over the sill. August's hands are warm and steady when they grab my waist, lifting me out and helping me to the ground. I shut my window almost all the way, leaving it cracked so I can get back in later tonight, before August and I quietly tiptoe through my backyard and out the side gate onto Oceanside Avenue.

"Where are we going?" I ask as he takes a sharp left, headed up toward the top of the cliff.

"I found a spot a few weeks back that I haven't had the chance to show you yet."

I follow him to the top of our street. There's an empty lot at the end of the cul-de-sac, thick with blackberry bushes. August continues through the gravel of the lot, stopping just in front of the brush. "We have to get through the blackberries. I started to tear them out," he says, pointing to a small clearing I can hardly make out in the darkness, "but be careful."

When he reaches back for my hand, I take it without a word, allowing him to lead me through. He stomps down on large branches so I can step over them without snagging my dress or scratching my ankles before tearing through thickets that stick out in the trail he created.

"I promise, it's worth it," he whispers.

"I trust you."

Finally, the sky opens above me as we pass through the bushes, and a vast cliffside appears. The soft green grass stretches endlessly beyond us, stopped only by the steep rocks that plummet into the ocean below. In the distance, the horizon goes on forever, late-night tides rocking gently beneath the glowing light of the crescent moon.

"Augustus," I gasp, spinning around to face him as I cover my mouth with my hand. "This is *insane.* How did you find this?"

He shrugs, hands in his pockets as he drops his head with a coy smile. Passing me, he strolls through the field of grass as he calls over his shoulder, "I was on a run one morning on that back road leading to the power plant. I noticed this field on the other side of the fence and realized there had to be a way to get to it from the neighborhood. It was likely just blocked by houses, so my next few runs, I went through the neighborhood instead and looked around until I found a way in."

"This is beautiful." I press on my heels, slipping out of each shoe before jogging up behind him. Looping my arm through his, I ask, "What have you been doing out here?"

"During the day, I come out here and draw sometimes. Or read." He lifts his head, and I follow his gaze toward the sky. "At night, I look at the stars."

All the air whooshes from my lungs as I take in the sheer number of stars sparkling above our heads.

"This cliff is high enough above the town that they're much clearer out here."

The sky is a never-ending vastness of darkness, brightened only by the sprinkling of sparkles across its canvas, the moon its centerpiece on the horizon. I let go of August, taking a few steps forward and turning in place as I absorb as much of it as I can.

It's calming somehow. I've always liked night more than day. I like the cover of darkness and the soft light of lamps and candles. I love the feeling of finishing an incredible book and looking at the clock to find it's three a.m., and you don't even care because you were lost inside another world where time is of no consequence. I like the way the world feels quiet and peaceful, and being awake in the midst of that is almost like a secret.

I love the night sky—you can't stare directly into the sun, but you can stare at the stars. You can study them as long and as intently as you want without fear they'll burn you.

"I'm sorry Zach stood you up," August says quietly, snapping me from my thoughts. "Leo was yelling at him in our group message, and when I realized what happened, I snuck out."

I drop my head and meet his gaze, finding some unreadable expression on his face. I'm normally good at reading him—I always know what's going through his mind—but every once in a while, he catches me by surprise when he puts his guard up.

"Thank you."

I watch his eyes track my body, starting at my lips, down to my feet, and back up again. "You look beautiful, Elena, and it's his loss to have missed it."

My throat swells, my earlier emotions and the sting of rejection rising once more. "I felt beautiful," I say, swallowing. "I felt...feminine, and you know that's a rare feeling for me."

He pulls his hands from his pockets and takes a step closer. "What were you looking forward to most?"

"Being pretty for once." I snort. "And the dancing. Slow dancing."

August nods, as if expecting that answer. He's quiet for a moment. His hand rises to cup the back of his neck as he takes a deep breath. Shaking his head slightly, he finally holds that arm out to me. "Do you want to dance now? At least get one out of that dress?"

The most genuine smile I've mustered all day creeps onto my lips. Nobody else gets me the way August gets me. I'd never ask a boy to dance. There is no one else I'd even admit those thoughts to.

About two years ago, I settled into this alternative, dark-girl persona. I like weird books I'm way too young to read, and I don't like having sleepovers. I don't play sports, and I hate concerts because they're too loud and crowded. I don't do great in social situations, and I force myself not to care about appearances because I'm afraid if I did, I wouldn't hold a candle to other girls. My favorite color genuinely is black—it's the only color I think elevates all others, but when I explain that, I get accused of trying too hard to be *different.*

Friends—and I use the word lightly—I've had in the past told me I was trying too hard to *not be like other girls*, and I never understood it.

I *want* to be like other girls. I don't know how, and nobody will teach me.

I don't want my only friends to be my fucking brothers, but I can't make myself try to connect with anyone else. Somehow, rejection from female friendships hurts worse than rejection from boys. It's like...I'm supposed to fit in with girls. I'm supposed to find solidarity and compatibility and support in them, but I'm too awkward and too dark and too...whatever the hell makes me so strange. Being unable to find my place in those spaces is a sharper sting than accusing a boy of being too stupid to keep up with me.

I'm too stubborn to conform, and despite it all, I like who I am. I know there are other girls out there who feel the way I do—I can even see it in some of the ones I go to school with—but trying to express that feels like an obstacle I'm not willing to overcome.

So, I stick to myself, to my brothers, because they'll always accept me. I let myself pine after Zach because I think he accepts me too, and August is my best friend because he accepts me most of all. He sees me deeper than the rest of them. He reads the pages of my soul that seem to be written in a language no one else understands.

Nobody else would ever ask me to dance because they can't imagine me wanting to, but Augustus Hayes hears the words I can never seem to say.

So I take his hand. "I do want to dance."

He smiles, pulling his phone out of his pocket with his free arm and, because he truly knows me better than anyone, he plays a Lana Del Rey song before dropping it onto the ground behind us. With the hand holding mine, he tugs me against him, snaking the other around my waist and resting it on my lower back. He opens his palm, and I let my fingers fall into the spaces between his.

August leads, moving us in circles as the slow, deep sounds of a harp and piano float around us. "You do look beautiful, Elena. All the time, but I'm sorry the whole world didn't get to see you tonight."

Something erupts in my chest at that, at the intense focus of his gaze clashing against my own. His eyes are so green, it feels like I'm staring directly into the depths of a gemstone. Stars dot the sky above his head, but they're nowhere near as bright as his eyes.

My heart rate drums in my chest, like it's part of the song playing around us.

I don't know what it means.

"I guess you're just the lucky one." I sigh, dropping my head against his chest, unable to face him any longer. His heart is thundering too, but the steady sound of it calms me.

August is warm and solid. He feels like safety, like the grass beneath my bare feet, soft and grounding. His hand at my back is comfort, like being wrapped in a blanket on a cold night, the peaceful heaviness of it. I could stay right here forever and I'd be okay.

It's different from when Zach touches me in the same place. Zach's touch is scorching. It's heat and thrill. It feels like something that doesn't belong to me, but I took it anyway—stolen and fleeting and desperate.

Zach feels like staring into the sun, but August feels like gazing at the stars.

"Why'd you come find me, Augustus? Why'd you ask me to dance?" I'm terrified of his response, but fluttering with anticipation for it too. This moment feels deeper than anything we've ever experienced, and I don't know what it means. I don't know if I want to, but I do know I don't want it to end.

He's quiet for far too long, so I lift my head and find him staring down at me. Something wars within his eyes, and just as I find myself lost inside them again, he whispers, "Because you're my best friend."

I smile, nodding before falling back into his chest. Besides the music playing, we're quiet. I match my breathing to the rhythm of his heart as we sway atop the coastal knoll, the moon and stars our audience.

August is the only real friend I've ever had, and I have nothing to compare this kind of connection to, so I tell myself that's the reason this moment—his touch—feels the way it does.

Friendship. That's all it is.

Chapter Five

Elena

Age Sixteen - August

"august" - Taylor Swift

Two knocks clang against my bedroom door, and I spin in my desk chair just in time—Zach leans against the hinges, my favorite smile on his face, his arms crossed with a massive bouquet of red roses tucked between them. "Happy Birthday," he drawls.

"Are those for me?" My voice comes out at least an octave higher than it should.

He only laughs, stepping into my bedroom and shutting the door behind him. "I wanted a second alone with you before the party." He strolls over to my bed, sitting on the edge as he tugs the leg of my chair and wheels me toward him. "I have a gift for you."

"You didn't have to get me anything," I murmur, hardly able to speak through the butterflies clogging up my windpipes.

My body feels like Jell-O when Zach grabs my chin and lifts my head, tucking a wild curl behind my ear. He flashes me his megawatt smile, and his chocolate eyes crinkle in the corners, causing my heart to hammer against my chest, begging to be let free and held by him. "Of course I had to get somethin' for my girl."

My girl.

My stomach lifts like I just took the drop off a roller coaster.

He hands me the flowers, so bright and fragrant. Normally, I'd prefer something less commercialized and less...red, but they're from him, and that's all that really matters.

"They're beautiful," I say, clutching the bouquet to my chest.

"That's not all," he chuckles, reaching into his back pocket and pulling out a small purple bag. Zach opens it, revealing a silver chain necklace with a small green gem at its center.

A mixture between a gasp and a squeal leaves my mouth as I clamp a hand over it. Zach holds the necklace up. "Peridot," he says, motioning for me to stand and turn so he can put it on. "It's your birthstone."

He spreads his legs as I spin and step between them, lifting my hair from my neck as he brings the chain around my throat, fingers warm where they graze my skin as he fastens it at my nape.

I turn to face him, brushing my hand over the gem. "It's stunning. I can't believe you remembered."

His hands come to my hips, inching beneath the hem of my T-shirt to caress my bare skin. My flesh lights on fire at the touch. "I even went to that crystal shop you love downtown. Told the lady working there it was for you, when your birthday is. She helped me pick it out." He smiles. "Oh, and"—reaching into his front pocket this time, he pulls out a small, folded piece of paper—"it came with this little card." Unfolding it, he reads aloud: "Known as the stone of compassion, peridot is believed to bring good health, restful sleep, and peace to relationships by balancing emotions and mind. This friendly, bright green stone has the uncanny ability to inspire eloquence and creativity; it also brings delight and good cheer."

"Hmm." I laugh. "Sleep, emotional balance, and delight

are things I'm lacking."

He shakes his head, chuckling as his lips whisper against my neck, "You're pretty damn close to perfect, actually."

He tosses the card onto my bedside table, his hand resuming its place on my hip as my fingers rake through his hair. "It's perfect, and so are the flowers." I lower my mouth to his. "And so are you."

He groans, grabbing me swiftly and tossing me onto my back as he crawls over me. He peppers kisses along my jaw, and those butterflies flutter out of my throat in the form of giggles as my heart pounds to a rhythm that could level buildings.

"I wish I had all day with you," he rasps against my throat.

"Me too," I whisper.

When he pulls back to look at me, his gaze is full of adoration and desire and something I want to call love, though I'm not sure I can, since he has never said the words.

"Let's make sure we get some time alone tonight, okay?" he asks breathlessly.

"Yes." I nod furiously, because it's impossible to want anything other than his feverish touch and his blazing eyes that look like love.

August

"Happy Birthday to my first and second favorite set of twins!" My brother raises his plastic cup, nodding toward Elena's chest before tossing her a wink.

Everett promptly throws a can of beer at Zach while Leo cups a hand around his mouth and yells, "Boooo."

Elena's blushing, glancing down at her chest, which admittedly does look fucking phenomenal beneath her low-cut tank. Everyone around is laughing, and I don't understand why. That joke wasn't funny. It wasn't witty or charming or even original. It's like Zach can do no wrong, and it drives me nuts.

Someone starts the music back up—"The Spins" suddenly blasting all throughout my house. I stumble through the wafting smoke and shouting teens, stepping out into my parents' backyard.

By pure coincidence, my mother was invited to some fundraiser in Los Angeles, so my parents decided to make a weekend of it. Zach took it as the perfect excuse to throw Elena and Everett a birthday party—except I know Elena would much prefer a quiet day with bookstores and brunch over an alcohol-infused sweat fest like this.

I also know Elena would hate having her body objectified in front of a large group of people, but somehow, if it's my fucking brother, she welcomes it.

I sigh, taking a sip of some concoction Leo mixed up that tastes like vodka, strawberries, and ass. I toss the drink in the grass and recycle my cup before sitting on the porch steps and stretching out my legs.

I thought Elena was done with Zach after he stood her up at prom—the same night she looked at me like she might want to choose me instead, and I fucked up by stating she was my *best friend.* She almost looked disappointed when I said that, like she was hoping I'd tell her she's so much more.

And I should have. I clammed up, and the words wouldn't come. After the moment passed, I hoped I'd get the chance to tell her how I really felt, but as soon as my brother showed up at her house the next day, begging for forgiveness, she was putty in his hands again.

And I've been fucked ever since.

Now, I sit outside alone while the girl of my dreams is

inside my house, sitting on my brother's lap, *his* hands on her waist, *his* face in her neck, *his* name she whispers.

My throat burns, my stomach sinks, and my jaw clenches. The envy so deep inside my bones, it's like they're breaking beneath the pressure of it, concaving and cracking and fucking killing me.

I suck in a sharp breath, face falling into my hands where they rest on my knees. The back door opens and closes behind me. "Oh. Sorry, I—"

"No, it's fine." I sigh, lifting my head to turn around. Abby Phillips stands behind me, her bright red hair falling off her shoulders, pale cheeks flushed and sprinkled with freckles, her blue eyes wide as she takes me in.

She swallows, slowly sitting down beside me. I meant it was fine she was outside; I didn't necessarily mean I wanted her to sit next to me, but I don't know how to say that.

My fingers drum awkwardly against my thigh as she says, "Hey, August."

"Hey, Abby."

"Um." She turns to face me, smiling softly. "How's the party?"

I shrug. "I don't love having my house invaded by people."

"I can imagine." She nods. "Sorry to be an invader."

"No, I—" I shake my head. "Sorry, I didn't mean it like that. You're fine." I stumble over my words. "You're great!"

I'm fucking stupid.

She giggles, hiding her face. "Thanks. Um, anyway...you're taking Mr. Adams's A.P. Literature class this term, right?"

"Yeah."

"I assumed. You're so smart." She smiles, biting her thumb. "Have you read *The Great Gatsby* yet? For the summer reading list?"

"I read *Gatsby* years ago, but I'll probably read it again before school starts up."

"Of course you've already read it." She laughs. "Well," dipping into the pocket of her jeans, she pulls out a napkin, "I thought...if you wanted to get together before the school year to talk about it, maybe read each other's reports? I..." She bites her lip, gently placing her hand, and the napkin with her phone number scribbled across it, on my thigh. "If you want to get together, you should text me."

Fuck. Does she mean what I think she does? Is that what this is?

My head whips sideways, meeting Abby's gaze head-on, and she's staring at my lips.

I clear my throat. "Thanks, Abby. I'll...uh... I'll definitely—"

The back door opens again. *Thank God.* It's not that I don't find Abby attractive. She's cute as hell. She's nice and smart, too. From what I hear, she's not crazy, and she hasn't fucked Everett, so that's a plus.

But when she put her hand on my thigh, I felt nothing—nothing compared to the way I know I'm capable of feeling when a girl touches me.

"Augustus!" Elena's voice chimes, and my entire body goes on alert, reminding me precisely just how much sensation I can experience from the presence of another person.

"I'll talk to you later," Abby murmurs, standing abruptly. Her footsteps pad up the steps, and the sliding glass door slams shut behind her as she re-enters the house.

"That was weird," Elena mutters, plopping down beside me, her drink sloshing over her cup and spilling down her hand. I track the droplets of Leo's fucked-up punch dribbling down her wrist, and I can't stop thinking about how much I'd be willing to stomach the toxic liquid if I was licking it off her skin.

"She's nice," I say instead.

Elena shrugs. She's definitely tipsy.

"Why did you run away?" she asks. "I missed you."

"Not a big fan of parties."

"But it's *my* party," she slurs.

"I thought you weren't a big fan of parties either."

"I'm a big fan of *you*." She giggles, throwing her arm around my shoulder and dropping her face into the crook of my neck. Her breath is warm, sending sparks down my spine as she continues, "Everett wanted a party, and I wasn't going to let him get all the attention on my fucking birthday."

That sounds more like her.

"Can I tell you a secret, Augustus?" she whispers in my ear, and the lower region of my body reacts in a way I really wish it wouldn't.

"Sure."

"I love you."

"That's not a secret."

She laughs, pulling away from me. Her brown eyes reflect light in a way that appears endless, like an abyss, which is fitting, considering I can't stare at her without getting lost.

"I love you, too, Elena."

"That's not a secret," she mimics me. "You're the only person I've ever told I love, besides my parents and my dumbass brothers. That's the secret."

"What about my dumbass brother?"

"Nope." She shakes her head. "But I think I might tonight." She bites her lip, and I wish I were the one biting it instead. But that reverie is ruined when I realize what she just said. She boops me on the nose. "Want to know another secret?"

I don't answer because I don't think I want to know this

one.

"I'm going to have sex tonight."

I didn't know it was possible to end a human life in six measly words, but I'm fairly certain I just fucking died.

"No, you're not," I snap.

She's drunk. She's drunk. She's drunk.

I repeat the mantra in my mind, convincing myself she didn't mean it.

Except Elena's brow furrows, and those beautiful caramel eyes catch fire. A serious expression takes over her face as she rears back. "Yes, I am? Who the fuck are you—"

"You're shit-faced, Elena." I take the plastic cup from her hand and set it on my other side, out of reach.

She rolls her eyes but doesn't fight me for it back. "I'll sober up beforehand." Raising three fingers in the air, she adds, "Scout's honor."

My stomach is in my goddamn throat, and I can't breathe. She just dropped bricks on my fucking chest, and she's smiling at me like it's no big deal, like she didn't just destroy me. Elena Ramos is a nuclear bomb, wreaking havoc on my entire world.

I grab both her arms, forcing her to look at me. Her mouth shuts and her eyes go wide with shock and alarm. "Elena, I am begging you." My voice shakes with desperation. "Do not give my brother—"

"Auggie!"

The sound comes abruptly from behind me, but before I have the chance to turn and find its source, a force rams into me, sending me tumbling down the steps of my back porch into the yard. There's a pressure on my back, and I'm too on edge to deal with bullshit right now. I'm fucking feral, I'm raging, and I want to set fire to everything around me.

I shove back against whoever pushed me down the stairs,

rolling over on top of them, cocking my fist, ready to break their face.

Leo's sad, blue, puppy dog eyes look up from beneath me, a pout on his face. "I'm sorry, dude, I'm sorry!" He holds his hands up in surrender. "I didn't mean to scare you. I just missed you. I couldn't find you anywhere."

"Dammit, Leo!" I shove at his chest, rolling off him.

He sits up, rubbing his neck before bursting with laughter. "Yeah, man. I don't even know which way is up right now, and I get kind of panicky when the room's spinning. I thought you went missing."

I roll my eyes, glancing back up at the porch. Everett's smothering his sister in a bear hug, muttering something about how he'd never want to share a womb with anyone else. They make a lot of womb jokes, and I think it's fucking odd, but I guess it's a twin thing.

Elena shoves him off, but she's laughing like our entire conversation just moments ago hadn't happened. She and Everett stand together and walk inside, and she doesn't spare a glance back at me.

I brush off my knees, grabbing Leo's arm to help him off the ground. "I'm fine. I'm not missing, but I need to take a fucking walk."

Leo follows my gaze through the door, and he nods as if he understands. "Don't stay away too long. I *will* call in an Amber Alert."

That earns a rough laugh from me, and I slap my friend on the back before I step away, stalking around the side of my house and out the back gate. Once my feet hit the pavement of our street, I run. I run until I'm numb, until I can no longer feel her touch, her breath on my neck. I run until I've all but forgotten the words she said to me, the secrets she told.

Yet one echoes in my head, keeping pace with the rhythm of my feet hitting the ground.

You're the only person I've ever told that to.

I love you. I love you. I love you.

The party had begun to die down when I returned home, only a few kids from school lingering around the kitchen. My brother and Elena were missing, and his bedroom door was shut. Leo and Everett were passed out on the living room couch, cuddling each other's feet. After taking a photo I'll definitely use for blackmail later, I not-so-politely kicked the loiterers out of my house before I cleaned up the kitchen and went to bed.

The issue with a daytime party is that it's only nine o'clock now, everyone around me passed out or MIA, and I'm stuck staring at my ceiling, a bullet train of images flashing across my mind of the girl I'm madly in love with and my older brother who doesn't deserve her.

I know I should put on some music. A movie. Anything to avoid a rogue sound coming from Zach's room across the hall. But I don't. It's almost like I'm searching for it, the confirmation, hoping the silence remains so I can convince myself nothing is happening at all. It's hard enough to know that on weekends, Zach sneaks through her bedroom window, or vice versa, and they sleep next to each other, but I allowed myself to live in blissful ignorance, pretending that's as far as anything ever went. I chose to walk through each day convinced she'd realize I was so much better for her, and she'd choose me instead.

I rub a hand down my face, taking a deep breath. If my two best friends weren't passed out on my couch, I'd have gone to their place tonight and crashed there. If I showed up on Monica and Carlos's doorstep right now, they'd let me in, no doubt. But they also might ask where their kids are, and I would then have to explain that two of them got shit-faced, and the other may or may not be actively losing her virginity.

I decide I need a glass of water—or maybe some of Leo's fucked-up punch. Maybe it'll kill me. At the very least, it'll help me pass out too. I need to escape my own mind for a little while. I throw myself out of bed, trudge to my bedroom door, and toss it open as I wipe at my heavy eyes.

I blink, adjusting my glasses as another door creaks open. My blurry vision focuses, and Elena stands in front of me. She gasps, stepping back suddenly before pausing.

"You scared me," she murmurs. I take note of her smeared eye makeup, the halo of distressed curls around her shoulders, and her bare legs beneath one of my brother's oversized T-shirts.

My heart, my stomach—all my internal organs, really—fall to the ground beneath me as I soak her in. Every confirmation I didn't want to receive is written plainly in the space between us, and I'm not sure I'll ever recover.

A prickling sensation spreads through my chest, the blade of a scorching knife tearing its way through my flesh.

"Are you still drunk?" I find myself asking.

She shakes her head. I study her eyes, finding them clearer than they were earlier. Despite the raging hatred for him flowing through my veins, I trust my brother enough to know that he wouldn't go there unless Elena was completely sober and willing.

"Are you okay?" I ask this time.

There is a soft smile on her face as she nods. I'm sure she assumes it's a reassuring expression for me, but she has no idea that she just ripped my heart from my body, taking my soul right along with it.

I can't bear another second of standing here across the

hall, staring at her like a soulless ghost with a hollow chest. "Goodnight, Elena," I murmur as I step back inside my room.

Her face falls as I shut my door in front of her.

Chapter Six

August

Age Fifteen - July

"illicit Affairs" - Taylor Swift

"I told you—I didn't fucking send that text"

"I saw the screenshot! It was your name."

"Okay? So she changed someone else's name to mine."

Elena rolls her eyes. "I'm so sure. Because Brooke Williams is *so* obsessed with you, she'd go so far as changing a name in her phone to convince me you're sexting her."

Leaning over the railing, I stare down at the whitecaps of the sea as they crash against the columns, wishing I was literally anywhere else. We've continued our stupid Saturday tradition of jumping off the pier, but Everett got caught with a girl in his room last week and had to mow lawns early this morning as punishment, and Leo is picking up his new friend, Darby, before meeting us down here.

Which means I'm stuck third-wheeling with Zach and Elena, and today seems to be an *off* day for them. They're constantly fighting—screaming and crying and slamming doors—whether that be lockers at school, the door to Zach's car, or his bedroom when she's at our house. They're like a natural disaster happening in front of your face that you're too stunned to look away from, and we're all collateral damage.

Elena cries in my arms, her brothers threaten to kick Zach's ass, and she swears she'll never speak to him again. Then, the next day, I catch them making out in his car during lunch, or I find her sneaking out of his bedroom early in the morning before my parents wake up.

I don't know why they thrive off each other's toxicity. I don't know why they continue to torture themselves. I don't know why I stand by and watch it happen, why I continue to comfort her after each falling out, knowing it's tormenting me too.

Today is no different. They're fighting, and I'm pretending I can't hear it as we wait for the rest of our friends to show their faces. Despite their lack of respect for my boundaries, they at least stay away from each other in the presence of Everett and Leo, who are both all too happy to pretend their best friend isn't fucking their sister and repeatedly breaking her heart.

"We were in a fight, Elena. I'm sorry, all right?"

"So you admit it then? You were sexting her."

"It was the same weekend you decided to make out with Derek at that party because you were pissed at me, so I don't understand what you're even upset about."

"You blocked my number!" she screams.

"And you sure moved on quickly."

A growl and a loud stomp signals Elena is about to start throwing a literal tantrum right here in public. Although, I don't know if I can blame my brother for that jab. I was pissed at her that night too. After a particularly ugly spat between the two of them, Zach blocked her number, and Elena tagged along with Everett to a house party, which ended with her straddling the lap of one of our classmates and sticking her tongue down his throat in front of everyone.

I might just be mad because I wish she would've used me instead, and I don't know what that says about the kind of person I am.

"You are such a fucking—"

"Hey, bitches!" Everett's voice rings out in the distance. It's his warning that he's arrived and Zach and Elena need to get their shit together. He doesn't address their fucked-up relationship so long as they keep it out of his face.

My head snaps up, and I catch him making his way down the pier from the Boardwalk, waving in our direction. *Thank God.*

Elena huffs, leaning back against the railing next to me and crossing her arms. Zach lets out a sigh of relief, and I damn near match it. "Sorry," Elena murmurs, shuffling closer to me.

"It's fine," I mutter.

"I hate fighting in front of you. I don't want you to feel like you're choosing sides." She loops her arm through mine, tugging us closer as she stares after me with soft, chocolate eyes.

I instantly melt. "I'm always on your side."

The insistence that I'm essentially a kid watching my parents bicker and not her best friend pretending he's not in love with her while constantly picking up her broken pieces—her fallen flower petals—is insulting.

She smiles, and a small laugh—the first she has let out all day—escapes her. Zach cuts me a glare, and if I have nothing else, I know I can make her smile in a way he can't. I may not set her life, her heart, or her body on fire the way my brother does, but I can make her feel safe. And, as always, I force it to be enough.

"Where's Leo?" Everett asks, jogging up to us. His eyes—the twin color to his sister's— dart between the three of us, taking note of the unspoken tension wafting through the air. Elena and Everett look so much alike, though he's about twice her size. Their parents say he stole all the height and Elena stole the beauty. I agree.

"Picking up the new girl," Zach says.

"He's so obsessed," Everett says with a chuckle.

"So obsessed," the rest of us agree in unison before busting up with laughter.

Leo stumbled upon the granddaughter of Diane Andrews, one of the Ramoses' neighbors, a couple of weeks ago. She's our age and staying with her grandmother for the summer. He seems to have become instantly smitten with the girl, because he hasn't shut up about her since, and now, he's begging her to hang out with us any chance he gets.

"Honeysuckle." Everett snorts. "Dumbest nickname I've ever heard."

"I think it's cute," Elena counters.

"Do you, Rosebud?" Zach smirks. Elena's middle name is Rose, and we all know she doesn't like it. She says being named after a flower is cliché.

"Fuck off."

"Rosebud. Yep. That's sticking." Everett nods. "Because it's your middle name, but also, you're like," he waves a hand up and down, referencing her stature, "small. It's perfect."

"I'll actually slit your throat," she snaps.

"Careful, she's thorny." Everett smiles tauntingly.

"More like—" Zach starts.

"Finish that sentence, and I'll slit *your* throat," Everett growls.

"C'mon, Augustus." Elena loops her arm through mine and drags me into Milo Chavez's house, our friends at our heels.

I'd much rather spend my Saturday night with a book, Elena next to me in the grass at our secret cliffside, but she's raging tonight, and this is the only time she likes to go to parties—she's angry, she wants to drink, and she wants to make my brother jealous.

She storms right through the front doors, not bothering to knock, revealing the roaring house party inside the giant mansion. I don't know Milo well, but clearly, he's rich. His house looks straight out of *The Fresh Prince of Bel-Air* or something: massive columns towering over the entry, a foyer with a double staircase leading to an upper landing.

A sea of bodies and a fog of smoke haze the environment as we enter, but Elena beelines straight for the kitchen. After filling both of our cups, she wordlessly grabs my hand and drags me into the backyard. A fire blazes in the pit at the center of the patio, and a few people mingle in the opulent swimming pool, but the music is a dull hum compared to the thunderous sounds inside the house.

"I know you hate loud music," Elena says as she takes a seat on an empty porch swing.

"Thanks," I respond, taking a sip of my drink. "But please, don't feel you need to babysit me all night. I can walk home whenever I want."

She rests her head on my shoulder. "I don't feel like I'm babysitting you, Augustus. I just feel better when you're around. I need the reminder I can have a good time without him."

"We always have a good time, no matter who else is around."

"I know." She sighs. "But Zach thinks we're boring, always reading or drawing or writing in our rooms and not socializing with other people. He thinks I rely on him to come out of my shell, that I hide inside it when I'm with you."

"Not everyone can be as social as my brother," I mutter. "That doesn't mean there is anything wrong with us. Our version of fun doesn't have to match his to make it valid, and you don't need to prove a goddamn thing to him."

"I know." She sits up on her knees, the swing rocking rapidly beneath us. Elena steadies herself, bracing her hands on my shoulders, leveling her face with mine. The flashing lights beneath the surface of the pool reflect across her face, casting her in waves of color. "But I want to prove it to him anyway."

"And that's why we're at this party?" I ask.

She nods. "And I'm not talking to him."

A dry laugh escapes me as movement in my periphery catches my eye. Abby Phillips steps into the backyard, heading toward the area where Elena and I sit. She stops short when she spots us, and I slowly lift my hand to wave at her. She rolls her eyes before stomping back inside.

"I see she hasn't forgiven you." Elena chuckles behind her cup.

"I told her it was going to be casual. I made myself crystal clear—I didn't want to hurt her feelings." *I didn't want to hurt her the way my brother hurts you*, I want to add.

"I think she took your virginity and thought that would mean something to you, even if you claimed beforehand that it wouldn't."

"I thought you said virginity was a social construct."

"Oh, it absolutely is." Elena snorts, taking a sip of her drink. "But I don't think Abby feels that way about it."

I sigh. I may have been quick to throw away my first sexual experience after the only girl I'd ever dreamed about gave hers to my older brother, but the last thing I intended was for Abby to feel used. We'd been study partners all last year, and I had a good time with her. When she expressed interest in wanting more, I explained I wasn't ever going to date her. I wouldn't be her boyfriend. That hadn't stopped her pursuits, though, and eventually, I gave in.

I needed to know if I could find what I craved from Elena in the arms of someone else.

And she never came close.

After a few months, I couldn't stomach it anymore, couldn't keep seeing Elena in my head every time I kissed Abby, every time I touched her. I cut things off, and she hates me for it.

"My little heartbreaker." Elena smiles, patting my cheek. Flames in the distance flicker in her eyes, setting them on fire, and as her full lips split into a wide grin, I think she's the most beautiful person I've ever seen. "I'm going to go check on Darby and see how she's doing."

She downs the rest of her drink before standing from the porch swing.

"You like her, don't you?" I ask with my own smile.

Elena thinks she's incapable of forming female friendships, but I can tell she has fallen in with the girl Leo brought into our group a few weeks ago. Elena's polar opposite in every way, Darby is blonde, innocent, and shy. I think Elena has loved taking Darby under her wing, and I think Darby likes being corrupted a little. I think both of them have had a hard time finding connections with people, and they recognize that struggle in the other.

"She's cool, but," she stretches her arms over her head, her Stevie Nicks T-shirt rising just enough to give me a glimpse of her stomach, "with how in love Leo is with her, I imagine she's going to be my sister-in-law someday, so I better take care of her." She winks at me before strolling inside.

I wait a few minutes, so it doesn't appear as though I'm following her, but sitting outside in the dark alone is uncomfortable. I figure I'll find the bathroom, and by the time I'm done there, Everett should be about finished with his hookup of the evening, and I can fuck around with him. I polish off my drink, tossing my cup into the trash as I head inside. I'm sure there are a million bathrooms in this house, but I go upstairs in hopes of finding one with less noise.

Turning left at the top of the landing, I make my way down the hall, opening and closing a few doors before I find one that must be a fucking bathroom—because I've now exhausted all the other options. I grab the handle and find it's unlocked, so I push it open with my shoulder.

Sure enough, there is a toilet in the corner next to a shower, a sink right in front of me. A brunette girl sits on said sink, her head tossed back against the glass, her lipstick smeared. It's my brother who stands between her legs, his mouth on her neck.

"You've got to be fucking kidding me."

My voice startles them both, and they jerk apart as Zach whips around.

"What the fuck! This room is occu—" His eyes go wide when he realizes it's me. "August—"

I shut the door, cutting off his words as it slams in his face.

I don't make it far down the hall before he's chasing after me. "August, wait! Wait, that wasn't what—"

"It was exactly what it looked like!" I yell, spinning to face him.

He stops in front of me, only a few inches taller than me now, whereas a year ago, he towered above me. He crosses his arms over his chest, muscles rippling beneath his Henley. He watches me for a moment, saying nothing.

I don't back down this time, not like before.

He might be my brother, but he's no good for Elena, and I'm tired of protecting him. She deserves to know what he's like, deserves to know *she* deserves so much better.

As if he reads that in my expression, his eyes soften. "I'm

sorry." Dragging a hand down his face, he continues, "Fuck. I'm sorry. I fucked up. I wasn't thinking."

"I don't care. That's not an excuse, and I'm not lying for you again."

This isn't the first time I've caught him. Every time, he swears it'll be the last, convincing me to keep his secrets from my best friend, from the girl of my dreams. Each time, I've done it, because despite how much he pisses me off, I love him. I look up to him. I search for the best in him, even if it feels like he's disappointing me time and time again.

Zach nods. "Just... Let me be the one to tell her. It shouldn't come from you." He rubs the back of his neck, pacing the hall. "I'll tell her, I promise. I'll tell her tonight. It was a mistake, I swear."

I know his emotions are genuine. I know, for how awful he is at showing it, he does care about Elena. I just can't wrap my head around why he continues to hurt her, or why she lets him.

"Why don't you guys just call it off if you're constantly doing this shit to each other?"

He pauses, sharp jaw ticking beneath stubble, thick brows furrowing with frustration, full lips parting as he sighs. "I have a shit way of showing it, I know." He shakes his head. "And you know what? So does she. But I do love her." He runs a shaking hand through his hair. "I know I'm bad for her, I know she's bad for me, but I love her, and that's more important than the rest of it."

"At what point does the love you receive stop being worth more than the pain you cause?"

He lifts his head, meeting my eyes. "When we've reached that point, I'll let you know. Until then, stay the fuck out of it, August."

Chapter Seven

Elena

Age Sixteen – July

"Love Me Anyway" - *Chappell Roan*

I'm pleasantly drunk, cuddled up next to my twin on a small couch around the fire pit.

I feel like I could fall asleep soon, but if there is one thing every teenage girl knows, it's that it's never safe to let your guard down at a house party. This is the point of the night when I'm stuck to one of my brothers, or to August, like glue, because they're not going to let another guy so much as look in my direction.

I'm wearing Everett's sweatshirt, and the fire's flames dance across my vision, sending sparks up into the night sky. The cracking of the wood drowns out the music and the conversations around me. It's peaceful.

Leo and Darby took off a while ago after some handsy motherfucker tried touching her while we were dancing. I've never danced at a party like that. I've never danced with anyone except August—and my dad. I've never had the courage. But Darby looked like she had never danced before either, like maybe she was also lacking in the bravery department. I thought maybe together, we'd figure it out, and we did.

Until some asshole tried groping her and Leo took her home.

I don't know what will become of them, what plans they're making, but I hope it works out. I think he's falling for her fast and hard, and I think she is too.

First love is so idyllic to me. It's rare and fleeting and almost miraculous. We're programmed to believe it's not possible, and yet we're surrounded by stories that romanticize it. We're all desperate to have a story like that of our own. The idea of finding someone young and growing with them, holding onto them as the world whips around us, running from our youth hand in hand—that's epic to me.

Maybe I romanticize it because I'm a victim of it myself; who knows?

But I see that kind of love in Darby and my brother, even after only a few weeks.

I hope that's exactly what it is for them, but with that hope lies certainty that if that girl ever hurts him, I'll never fucking forgive her.

"I need to talk to her. Now."

"She's asleep, asshole."

Voices break me from my thoughts, and I realize only now that my eyes are closed. I must've been teetering on the verge of unconsciousness. I slowly open them, lifting my head from Everett's shoulder and blinking as my hazy vision clears. The glow of the fire is blocked by Zach's silhouette, who's bent down in front of me, caution in his brown eyes.

He looks like he's wrapped in a halo of sunset colors—or rising out of the depths of hell to wreak havoc on my life. Could go either way, really.

"Hey, Rosebud." He smiles at me mischievously. "Care to take a walk?"

"You don't have to, Lele," my brother mutters from beside me.

Zach glares at him, and I roll my eyes at them both.

"I guess." I yawn, sitting up and stretching as I toss the blanket from my shoulders onto Everett. Zach grabs my hand and helps me off the couch, taking me to the far end of the sprawling back lawn and away from the rest of the partygoers.

There's a bench sitting within a thicket of rose bushes, lit only by the moonlight this far from the house. Zach doesn't let go of my hand as he sits down, tugging me with him. His breathing is unsteady, and he refuses to make eye contact with me.

If this were the first time we'd had a conversation like this, I might be unable to read the signs, but unfortunately, I know exactly what he's about to say.

He reaches an arm across my lap, grabbing my outer knee and turning it so I'm facing him, my legs between his. His hand slowly drags up my arm, leaving embers in its wake, the way only his touch can. He cups my cheek, brushing a thumb across it as a soft smile accents his beautiful face.

"You know how much I care about you, right?"

My heart sinks like a discarded corpse, drifting toward the ocean floor. I'm the victim, and Zach Hayes is the primary suspect in the murder of my fucking soul. My throat swells, and tears already sting my eyes.

"Just say it, Zach. Get it all out there." I wave my hands, readying myself for the word vomit he's about to spew across my hollow chest. He's ridding himself of the guilt, coating me in my own heartbreak.

"I kissed someone tonight. I'm so fucking sorry, Elena."

Tears slip down my cheeks, but I don't remember giving them permission to fall. They're not representative of how I truly feel, because all I am is fucking angry. I'm angry, tired, and drained.

I wish this were the first time I was having this conversation with him, or better yet, I wish the first time I had this conversation with him, I had walked away. Back then, I forgave him, and that only served as my approval to let it happen again.

I know I deserve better than this—mind games and unbroken wheels of heartache.

But Zach Hayes looks into my eyes, and all I see is the depths of his own. I see his hurt and his remorse, and I remember he doesn't look at those other girls the way he's looking at me right now. Whoever he kissed tonight, he has already forgotten. He can't forget me.

I don't know why we can't be uncomplicated, but if we were, we wouldn't be us. A fire blazes under my skin when he looks at me like this. When we fight, when we kiss. It's a fire I didn't feel when I kissed that other boy a few months ago, and I'm so afraid if I lose Zach, I'll go my whole life searching for that fire in someone else, only to never find it.

I want first love. I want idyllic and rare and miraculous, and most of the time, Zach only leaves me with the feeling that this is fleeting. Still, I can't stop myself from desperately holding out for the possibility that we could be all those other things, too.

I didn't choose to fall in love with him, and the revolving door of chaos that we tend to be stuck inside may not be what I envisioned love feeling like, but I have to believe that it all means something more. I fell into him without warning and without choice, but he eclipsed my life, and now I revolve around him like the sun.

The sun may be more powerful than the Earth, but the Earth can't exist without it, so what choice does it have? What choice do *I* have?

"Elena, can you say something to me?" he asks, holding my

face—my heart and my pain—in the palms of his hands.

"Why?" is the only word that comes out of my mouth.

As he searches my face in an attempt to read the emotions I don't normally keep from him, he simply sighs. "Sometimes, I have to risk losing you to remember I love you."

That's like a searing knife right through the center of my soul.

"What the fuck does that mean?" I shove his hands off me, creating distance between us so I can breathe. His presence drowns me, makes my head swim, and leaves me unable to think straight.

I thought I was numb for a moment, too used to this carousel with him to feel, but after what he just said, my rage is more potent than ever.

"I don't know." He shakes his head, running a hand through his hair. "I was trying to be honest. I guess I... I want to feel like you're fighting for it, Elena. Fighting for me and for this." He waves a finger between us. "When you choose my brother over and over and over again, it doesn't feel like you're fighting for us, and then I wonder what the point even is."

My head feels like it might actually explode, and I think I might like it if it did. We're out here alone in the dark, and if he had to walk back into that party with my brain matter splattered across his body, he'd definitely go down for my murder.

The fucking audacity.

"All I ever do is choose you!"

"It doesn't feel that way to me!"

My head falls into my hands as I palm my eyes, trying to rid myself of the tension headache this fucking asshole caused. "How did you kissing someone else end up being my fault?"

"It's not. I fucked up. I should've talked to you." Zach drags a hand down his face, falling back onto the bench. "But I don't think you understand what it does to me when you hold my brother's hand or ignore me to be with him instead. You choose him. You always choose him."

I did choose August. I mean, I stumbled upon him too, but I could've had one conversation the day we met and never spoken to him again. That day, I saw myself in another person for the first time ever. Someone who loved art and reading and quiet, the way I do. Someone who didn't question why I'd climb a neighbor's tree to pick purple flowers or why it's so hard for me to make friends.

When I recognized myself in him, I *chose* him.

I revolve around Zach like he's the sun, but I rely on August like he's the atmosphere.

I didn't choose to fall in love with Zach, but I make an intentional choice every single day to choose August as my best friend, and the truth is, I'm not sure who I need more.

But I do know when Zach breaks my heart, August heals it.

If I walked away from my friendship with August, I don't know if Zach would replace it. I don't think he could fill that hole—I don't think he'd want to.

"He's my best friend," I say.

Zach lifts his head, and the moonlight shines against his brown eyes like opalescent spheres, like stars in the sky. "Is that all he is to you?"

"Yes," I breathe, sitting down next to him. "You might be the dumbest person I've ever met."

He huffs a laugh. "Rude."

"For four years, I've been infatuated with you. I've chased you, I've cried over you, I've forgiven you every time you've hurt me. I gave you my first kiss, my first...everything."

"You said virginity is a soc—"

"Yeah, I know what I said." I smile at him, though I don't

feel it. "But my body is a fucking temple, and you're the only one who has ever touched it. You're welcome."

He turns to face me, lifting a hand to the back of my neck. His fingers knot in my hair, thumb brushing against my nape, sparks rushing down my spine. The touch I fear I'll never find elsewhere.

Zach says nothing, pulling my head toward his and dropping his mouth to mine. I let him kiss me, and I kiss him back because I know we're both desperate for one moment that doesn't feel like anger or tragedy. We need that fire running through our veins to be ignited by something other than pain.

But as his lips move against me, as I taste his tongue, I remember I'm not the only girl who has experienced this from him tonight.

I place a hand on his chest, pushing him back. "I can't."

"Elena." His voice breaks. "C'mon. Don't be like that right now. I thought we talked it out?"

"It tastes like you've been in someone else's mouth tonight, Zach. I can't move past that right now."

He scoffs. "That's a little dramatic, no?"

"No." I stand from the bench. "Weaponizing my friendship with your brother doesn't forgive the fact that you cheated on me. Again."

I turn around to walk away, tears welling in my eyes once more, realizing how manipulative he truly is, masking his mistakes and spinning our conversation so I'd forgive him easier. I didn't realize until I was kissing him again how he orchestrated the entire conversation to end exactly the way he desired.

"You're acting fucking childish, Elena!"

"Funny you say that, considering you treat me like a toy you don't want to share." I stop, glancing back at him. "I'm going home. I'll talk to you later."

I watch him stand, but I begin walking again before I can give him the chance to catch up. "If you're going to act like that, don't bother calling me."

I roll my eyes, lifting my middle finger in the air as I disappear into the night. I round the side of Milo's house and head down his massive driveway, down the hill that heads back toward town and home.

I'm halfway there, strolling through the quiet darkness, when Leo sends a message in the group chat letting us know we should be scarce tonight—our mom caught him sneaking in after dropping Darby at home. He told her we were both sleeping at the Hayes' house to try and save our asses, though I'm sure she'll know we're full of shit.

Nobody sees right through us like our mother. She's a fucking force.

Suddenly, my phone vibrates in my hand, and I glance down to see Everett's name flashing on the screen. I swipe to answer it, and before I can greet him, his voice roars from the other end, "Where are you?"

"I'm walking home."

"By yourself?"

"Yeah."

My brother grumbles under his breath, and I hear shuffling on the other end of the line before he shouts, "Hey, bitch! Why *the fuck* did you let my sister leave in the middle of the night by herself when she's been drinking? What is wrong with you?" I swear, I hear what sounds like some kind of slap before someone groans.

"Fuck you, Everett. Don't fucking touch me." Zach's voice is muffled in the background.

"Elena, stay where you are. I'm going to make this piece of

shit come get you. You cannot be out running around town by yourself in the middle of the goddamn night. Are you crazy?"

"You didn't care when it was August and Leo leaving the party," I snap back.

"Leo wasn't alone, and he took an Uber! August left early," he counters before adding, "and neither of them is my baby sister!"

"I'm four minutes younger than you. Calm the fuck down."

"Four minutes younger but a foot shorter."

I roll my eyes. "I'm fine, Everett. I'll let you know when I get home. I'm almost there."

"Leo said not to go home."

"I don't care," I say, even though that's not where I'm going.

"Stay on the phone with me until you get there, okay?" Everett asks.

"I'll go get her. This is ridiculous," a voice that doesn't belong to my brother echoes through the phone. "Why do you put yourself in these situations, Elena? You always have to cause such a scene, and it's the people who fucking care about you who get caught in the crossfire like this."

"I won't get in the car with him, Everett. I won't."

"He's already walking in the house." My brother sighs defeatedly, like he's as tired of mine and Zach's bullshit as we are. "What happened? Do you want me to tell Leo to sneak back out and come get you himself?"

I love my twin more than just about anyone else on this planet, but the overprotective audacity is getting on my goddamn nerves.

"God, no! I will text you when I get home. *Fuck*."

I hang up before he can argue with me, and suddenly, I'm running.

I know I'm probably still drunk. I'm overwhelmed and

sad, a little scared now that I realize it's so dark and so late. I'm stupid for taking off on my own. I hate the way Zach treats me like a petulant child, and that my brothers think I can't take care of myself. They treat me like I'm some emotional, impulsive, reckless girl they can't get rid of.

I'm running because I don't want Zach to catch up with me. I don't want to see him right now. I'm running because I need to get off the street. I'm running because I want the burn in my chest to be from something other than my heartache.

And I don't run home.

I run right up to the house on Hillside Road with the jacaranda tree in its front yard, to the window on the end with the soft glow illuminating the curtains.

I softly knock, knowing he's still awake. A moment later, the window opens, and August's face appears. The burn in my chest recedes, and I don't know if it's because I've now caught my breath or because I'm looking into the eyes of the one person who never makes me feel bad about who I am.

"Are you okay?" he asks.

Tears start falling again, and it's all I can do to shake my head.

He nods toward his room, beckoning me inside. I brace my arms on the sill and hoist myself through the window. He grabs my waist as he helps me in—his touch always soft and warm. It's not fire, but embers.

"What happened?"

I shake my head again, looking around. The lamp on his desk is on, his chair pulled out, and his sketchbook open to a rendering of a snake halfway done.

"Is that a tattoo you're designing for someone?" I ask, changing the subject.

August has been into drawing his entire life, but last year, after watching a documentary about it, he found an interest in designing tattoos. He began doing stick-and-poke work on my brothers and on himself before he found some second-hand equipment online that he now hoards in his garage away from his parents.

Some people at school caught on, and he has this whole underground operation going now. The craziest thing about it is that he's incredibly talented; you'd never be able to tell the tattoos were done by a fifteen-year-old kid.

"Yeah, for Tyler Childers," August says.

I nod, turning to face him and attempting to smile, but for some reason, it only makes me cry harder. August pulls me into his arms, cradling my head. He smells like the laundry detergent his mother uses to wash their clothes mixed with his deodorant, which is different from his brother's. Hugging him feels different, too. It feels like I'm being understood, like he's telling me he sees me and it's okay for me to feel this way.

My head fits perfectly into his shoulder. When we met, I was taller than he was, but over the years of our friendship, he has grown to tower above me, and I'm thankful for that now. It makes me feel even safer.

"Can I sleep here tonight?" I murmur against his chest.

"Of course. I can sleep on the couch."

"That's not what I meant."

He pulls back, studying my face intently as he looks down at me. Swiping a thumb beneath my eyes to clear my tears, August says quietly, "My brother won't like that."

"I don't care," I whisper. "You're my best friend, and you're the only person who makes me feel safe right now."

I don't just mean physically. I mean my soul. There is a bone-deep awareness when I'm with August that I can be exactly who I am and be accepted. He doesn't treat me like a child, like I'm naïve or immature or fragile. He doesn't belittle my dreams or my interests; he shares them. He doesn't make me feel like I have to mask my emotions, no matter how big they may be. It's my soul that's safe with him, and I think maybe that's why I choose him.

My soul longs for Zach, but it's not safe with him.

I don't want to think about what that means or how badly it hurts right now. No, I just want to fall asleep blanketed in warmth and security, and that's right here in August's bed, with him beside me. We don't touch, but we never touch that way.

I won't pretend there aren't weak moments when I think about how that might feel, because I do, even though I know it's wrong. But right now, it's not his touch I need—it's his presence.

August silently nods, walking over to his dresser and pulling out a pair of sweatpants and a T-shirt for me to change into. As he hands them to me, he gruffly says, "I'm going to go get you some water and some ibuprofen. You'll be hungover tomorrow. You can change while I'm doing that."

"August?" I ask as he quietly opens the door, pausing on the threshold. "Thank you." *For always taking care of me. For accepting me. For being my other half.*

He turns around, his gemstone eyes bright with conviction behind his glasses. He smiles softly, and it somehow seems sad. "I'll do anything for you, Elena."

He leaves the room, and as I'm changing, I see his phone light up on his desk beside his sketchbook. And because I'm nosy as hell, curious about who would be texting August at two in the morning, I check the notification. It's his brother's name flashing across the screen:

I assume she's with you?

Don't forget what I said.

August's door opens a moment later, and I quickly turn back around, pretending I hadn't seen Zach's message. He hands me a glass of water and two pills. I take them while he pulls back the comforter on his bed and crawls into the right side, the side he always sleeps on. I walk to the left—my side. The side I lie on while we're reading, the side I sneak into when I fight with his brother in the middle of the night and need a safe place to sleep.

He flips off the light, and we both lie on our backs, staring at the ceiling. It feels as if the words hanging between us penetrate the darkness, but we're both too afraid to voice them.

I'm fighting the urge to reach for his hand and feel his skin.

I think he's fighting those urges too, and as I hear the click of a lock toward the front of the house, the echo of quiet footsteps, and a door shutting across the hall, reminding me of the third variable in this fucked-up equation, I've never been more uncertain.

Chapter Eight

August

Age Sixteen - November

"Guilty As Sin?" - Taylor Swift

"My brain isn't working, Augustus," Elena mutters from behind me where she sits on my bed.

"It must be working a little, or you wouldn't have been able to say that."

I can practically hear her rolling her eyes at that, even though I'm not looking at her. I smile to myself, shading in the mountains that stretch across my sketchbook page. I've been working on my landscape skills because as more kids from school ask me for tattoos, I'm finding just how many people want that kind of artwork permanently marked on their body.

Not that I'm complaining. I'm making enough money to cover the cost of my license as soon as I graduate high school. I also met an incredibly skilled artist in San Diego this past summer who offered me an apprenticeship once I turn eighteen. It feels good to be the only person my age who knows exactly what I want to do with my life. Well, except maybe Leo. I don't think he's capable of being anything but a professional surfer, so it's a damn good thing he's the best at what he does.

I push back from my desk and spin my chair, taking in the sight of Elena. She's cross-legged on my bed in a worn-out Vans T-shirt and a pair of shorts, her dark curls falling around her shoulders as she stares down at the notebook in her lap, tapping her pencil against the page.

"Why isn't your brain working?"

"I forgot words."

"Well, there's three right there."

She lifts her head, and despite the glare on her face, I see the amusement in her eyes. There's just enough that I'm able to dodge the pencil that comes flying at my head a moment later, laughing as I get out of my chair and flop onto the bed beside her.

"I'm kind of over writing poems," she says.

"Yeah?"

Elena has been writing poems for years. Sometimes, she writes them about us—her brothers and myself, and I assume Zach too—but she never gives them to us directly. She slips them into my backpack when I'm not looking or leaves them under my pillow. She writes them in Italian, and while I can't read them, I have no doubt they're filled with the most beautiful words I'd ever read. I keep every single one in a box inside my nightstand, right alongside all the drawings I've made of her beautiful face that I know I'll never show her.

"I might want to write a book." She tilts her head at me, biting her lip. "Is that stupid?"

"No," I say immediately. "That's amazing. Fantasy? Romance? Thriller?" Elena reads all those genres, and I could see her writing any of them, or all of them at once.

"Romance, but maybe with some elements of suspense? Like an episode of *Criminal Minds*, but how fun would it be if the horrible villain was actually just misunderstood, and in the end, they get the happy ending?"

I laugh. "You do have a ton of empathy for the villains in those shows. You're always so eager to figure out what shaped them into who they are."

She shrugs, looking almost embarrassed.

"I think that sounds like a lot of fun, Elena. I think if there is anyone out there who could do it, it's you."

"I don't know. It's stupid."

"It's not." I lightly place my hand on her thigh, enough to comfort but not enough to show her just how badly I really want to touch her. I'm always riding that line. "You should write what you're compelled to write. It means you have something to say, which means there might be someone out there who needs to hear it, even if you haven't found them yet." I shrug, turning over on my back to stare at the ceiling. "Or, worst-case scenario, it sucks, and the only people who'll ever read it are you and me."

Her pretty face interrupts my view a moment later, hair falling like a curtain as she drops her head to look at me. "Why do you assume I'd let you read it?"

I roll my eyes. "Of course you'd let me read it. You need my opinion."

"You wouldn't be honest. You'd tell me it's great even if it wasn't."

"No," I argue. "I'm always gonna be your number one fan, but if you wrote a book that truly sucked, I'd never let you publish it. I wouldn't let you embarrass yourself like that, even if it hurt your feelings."

She snorts, and I'm still staring at the ceiling as her weight leaves my bed. "All right, let's go then."

I sit up and she's standing in front of my doorway, a perfect hip kicked out against it as she crosses her arms. "Go where?"

"Well, I need some inspiration. I'm never going to start writing a novel if I'm just sitting here in your room. We need to run around in the dark, be weird and creepy. I need to get into the mind of a villain."

"You're not asking me to like...kill someone, are you? I mean, I'd definitely help you bury a body, but I'd hope it'd at least be manslaughter."

"Augustus," she mutters, caramel eyes rolling. "No, I just need to get out of the house. Let's go."

I laugh, getting up and following her. Both of our parents are out in Carlsbad tonight, watching Zach and Everett play football. Elena and I don't normally attend the away games.

Leo didn't go tonight either, but he's at home by himself. All he tends to do nowadays is sulk and surf. Despite only knowing her for a couple of months, and knowing it was just for the summer, Darby did a number on him when she went back to Kansas in August without saying goodbye. He fell way too hard for her, way too fast, even going so far as to make me tattoo her name on his chest.

She got a tattoo for him, too, and the worst part is, she wouldn't let him look at it.

She left, and he never saw the dainty scroll I inked across her hip with his nickname. I feel weird telling him about it now. I've decided it's not my place, so we don't talk about it. We don't talk about Darby at all. Elena hates her for leaving Leo, but I think she was hurt by it herself, too. Darby was the first real girl friend she'd ever had, and she didn't say goodbye. She just disappeared.

We tried having an intervention for Leo last month because he wouldn't stop writing Darby letters and leaving them on her grandmother's doorstep, despite the fact that Darby hadn't returned a single one. He's still wearing the necklace she gave him—a simple chain with a gold ring attached to it—around his neck. We urged him to move on, even tried setting him up on dates. He wouldn't have any of it, told us not to bring her up again, and isolated himself until we finally stopped.

Their mom, Monica, said that as long as he was eating, surfing, attending school, and not doing drugs, we needed to give him space to mend his broken heart on his own. She promised he'd be okay eventually, but she looked sad when she said it, like she wasn't sure if she believed herself.

So we give him the space he needs for now, but I miss him being around more often.

I don't have to ask Elena where we're going; within ten minutes of stepping out my door, we're crawling through the shrubs we've spent two years clearing a pathway between, and emerging onto our secret cliffside.

It's a new moon tonight, so it's darker than usual, but the stars are brighter than ever.

"The stars look *insane* tonight," Elena gasps, voicing my thoughts.

She runs ahead of me before plopping down in the center of the field and lying on her back. I take my time walking toward her, admiring how beautiful she looks when she's invested in something. She goes through small phases of hyper-fixations, whether it's crystals, tarot reading, a certain book series, or her most recent one, astrology.

Once she shows that kind of interest in something, though, it never really goes away. She has an incredible talent for remembering everything. She could've read a random fact about Scorpios on the internet two years ago, and she'll still use it to judge someone now.

Luckily for me, she says my Taurus moon and her Pisces moon make us compatible, though her Aries rising and my Aquarius rising could make us butt heads.

I silently lie down beside her.

"Can you find Leo for me?" she asks, pointing at the sky.

I have a better knack for finding the constellations than

she does. She says the stars morph together in the sky and she can't make out their shapes unless I point to them for her.

I tilt my head up, tracing the stars until I find the nine dots that make up the symbol of the lion. I raise my hand, pointing to the north. "There."

I turn to her, watching her eyes squint as she attempts to follow my arm. "I can't see shit."

Laughing, I reach into my pocket and pull out the fine-point pen I was shading with at home. I can't remember why I tossed it in my pocket when we left—what I thought I'd need it for—but I'm glad I have it now.

I roll up, moving into a cross-legged position at Elena's side. "Give me your arm."

She doesn't question me, doesn't even take her eyes from the sky as she tosses her forearm across my lap. I press dots into her skin with the pen, connecting them to form the constellation. She giggles as my pen slides along her arm, and I realize she must be ticklish there.

I wonder if my brother knows that.

I finish the constellation, placing her hand back in her lap. "Raise your arm and then find the constellation in the sky that matches the one I just drew."

Her arm shoots in the air, a bright smile spreading across her face as she studies her skin and the sky. "You are a genius, Augustus." She traces two fingers over the ink. "This would be cool as a tattoo. When are you going to tattoo me, by the way?" Elena turns her head, shooting me an unconvincing scowl.

"Your body is too pretty for me to practice on," I say before I can think hard enough to stop myself. *Fuck*. "I mean—I don't..." I groan, face flushing with embarrassment. "I'm not going to risk scarring you forever in the same way I don't care if I accidentally give Leo or Everett a fucked-up tattoo."

I stare at my hands, feeling stupid.

"Augustus," she says, waiting patiently until I find the courage to meet her gaze. Elena's smiling, and if I didn't know better, I'd think I was making her blush. But I do know better. It's my brother who makes her blush. "I know what you meant," she continues, turning back toward the sky with that same smile on her face. "Plus, we both know you love my tits."

I groan, wiping a hand down my face as she laughs at me.

She has no embarrassment when it comes to her body or the way she catches me looking at it. I have infinite levels of humiliation that my best friend is well aware of how attracted I am to her.

After a moment of silence, Elena says, "I want matching tattoos."

"That worked out poorly for Leo." I sigh, lying down next to her, the grass beneath me soft, the sky above vast and endless.

"Don't worry, Augustus." She smiles sweetly. "I'm not an evil succubus here to suck out your soul, force you to fall in love with me, and then disappear without a trace." I watch her from my periphery as she looks toward the stars again. "Plus, you're my best friend. I'm never going to look at a representation of you on my skin and wish it wasn't there."

I stare after her, speechless. Only three thoughts filter through my mind as I get lost in the depths of her endless brown eyes:

God help Darby Andrews if she ever shows up in town again.

I'm already in love with her, have been all my life, whether she forced it or not.

I want her on my skin, too.

Elena pats the ground on her other side. "Come sit over here."

"Why?"

She raises her opposite hand. "I want you to practice. Give me a tattoo on this arm."

"What do you want?" I ask.

"Something that reminds you of me."

I smile to myself; it's not the first time I've thought about tattooing Elena's skin. I fucking dream about it, in fact. The idea of permanently marking her gives me a sense of satisfaction I'm desperate for. If I had it my way, I'd tattoo my name on her right now.

But she's not mine. I wasn't kidding when I said I don't want to fuck up her skin for eternity. My skill level is phenomenal for my age and experience, but it's not good enough for her yet. She's too perfect—too pristine—and the first time I ink her, I'm going to make damn sure it turns out as flawless as she is.

I sit up and crawl over her, trying not to think too hard about the way it feels when her thigh grazes my groin. I suck in a sharp breath as her body presses beneath mine, because that's another thing I only allow myself to imagine in my dreams.

Late at night, when I'm in bed, sometimes even when I know she snuck into my brother's room across the hall, I fantasize about her wrapped up in my sheets instead, my hands on her hips, my lips on her neck. I dream of her on top of me, of the way her body moves. What sounds she might make when I do something right, how eager I'd be to let her teach me how to please her and only her.

I hit the ground next to her hard enough to rock me from my reveries, and I find my mind drifting toward anything that'll remove the evidence of my thoughts from my body. The joggers I'm wearing leave nothing to the imagination. Elena's not looking at me, but her arm swings out to the side as she places it in my lap, and I have to roll out of the way.

She was heading straight for my hard-on, and that would've ruined the night for both of us. I groan as I tumble onto my back, dodging her touch. Elena perks up at my movement, head whipping sideways to look toward me. "What are you doing?"

"There was a bug." I swipe at my thighs, inconspicuously hiding my dick before sitting up again. She gives me an unconvinced look before tossing her arm onto my lap again. I grab the pen, tapping it against her skin.

Part of me wants to draw butterflies because that's what I felt in my stomach the day I met her, what I still feel every time I make her laugh. Or possibly a human heart with a hole through its center, blood seeping down the sides, because that's how it feels every time I see her with my brother. Stars because it feels like I exist among them when I'm with her. Books or poems because those remind me of her, too. I consider roses because that's her middle name, but I quickly scrap the idea because I know it's not her favorite flower.

She told my brother that before, too, but it was a bouquet of roses he gave her on her birthday. She pretended she loved them, and I know she didn't.

I picked her a bouquet of violets from the very field we're sitting in now. This is our secret place, a haven we don't share with anyone else, but also, I know violets are her favorite flower. It's a fact she has shared with my brother countless times, but he doesn't bother to remember.

The design flows from my fingertips then and, deep in concentration, I don't know how much time passes in silence, but neither of us seems to mind. I'm focused on creating art on her skin; she's focused on the movement of the sky. It's this peaceful silence, this comfortable darkness we always find together. The world is quiet when I'm with her. Nothing else exists beyond us and the moment we're in.

It's what convinces me we're meant to be.

That's a thought I keep locked deep inside, because at the end of the day, no matter how safe she feels with me, how much I make her laugh, or how desperate I am for her, she belongs to someone else.

But the most authentic version of her is mine, even if it's only friendship, and I'll never risk that. I'll never take away her safe place, her comfort and her peace, even if it means I'm forced to live in the reveries that only exist inside my mind.

"Finished," I say, clicking the pen closed and placing her arm back across her body. Her eyes were closed, but they fly open as she lifts her hand and admires my work.

"Violets?" she asks, turning to smile at me.

"They're your favorite."

"I love that about you," she says. "You remember everything about me."

"Nothing about you is easy to forget."

"I love you, Augustus." She smiles, tracing her fingers over the flowers along her arm.

"I love you too, Elena," I respond, knowing the words are the same, but we're saying two completely different things.

Chapter Nine

Elena

Age Seventeen - March

"that girl" - Kenzie Cait

"Dad, I'm so sorry, but I am not going to dance with you out here in the middle of the pier." My father laughs, brown eyes crinkling at the corners as he walks backward with a hand extended toward me. I stop, sighing. "I say this with so much love and respect, but you do know you're incredibly embarrassing, right?"

"Isn't that my job, *Corazón*?"

"*Trattienilo e basta, ok? Non si arrenderà finché non ballerai con lui*," my mom mutters in Italian from behind me. My brother laughs beside her.

My dad hates that Everett and I decided to take Italian in high school so we could learn to speak it with my mom. Her family comes from Sicily, and she used to take lessons from her grandmother when she was a girl, but after she passed away, my mom lost the knowledge. When Everett and I chose Italian for our foreign language requirement, my mom began taking online classes alongside us.

My dad did not.

So, it's our preferred way of talking about him in front of his face, knowing he can't understand most of what we're saying.

I huff an exaggerated sigh, taking my dad's hand and letting him spin me in circles, right in the center of the Pacific Shores Pier for any passerby to watch.

"You love this song, baby." He chuckles.

He's not wrong about that part. "Linger" by The Cranberries is one of my long-time favorites. My dad introduced me to it himself. He exclusively plays music made before the year two thousand in the garage he owns, and, having spent most of my afternoons at Ramos Automotive as a kid, I have a pretty well-rounded knowledge of it all.

My dad has this thing he loves to do. If he hears a song he feels like dancing to, he just dances. He doesn't care where he is or who's watching. I've seen him get down everywhere, from the airport terminal, grocery store aisles, to the DMV. My mom entertains it, my brother thinks it's funny, and I'm highly embarrassed about it, but it's really my only complaint about the guy. He's a perfect father in all other aspects, including a lack of shitty dad-jokes, which I appreciate.

Everett and I had lunch with our parents at the Seaside Sunset, a restaurant at the end of the pier. We're all so busy now between Everett's shifts at the garage, Leo meeting with agents and scouts, my new job at Harbor Coffee, and the three of us finishing up our senior year of high school, we don't have dinner much as a family anymore.

Once a week, we do our best to sit down with our parents for a couple of hours and eat together, though today, Leo was invited to train with an Olympian surfer from Los Angeles, and he couldn't turn down the opportunity.

Sometimes, it feels like the whole world is waiting for my brother to turn eighteen in May so they can descend on him like a pack of wolves. I know he's going to do amazing things. He's already setting records and making a name for himself in professional surfing, but I fear he'll get taken advantage of, and the worst part about all of it is, he doesn't seem to care if he does.

Everett and I give our parents hugs as we take a left off the pier down to the water, and they take a right toward the Boardwalk where they parked the car. We navigate down the beach until we find where Leo left our stuff. As we reach the neon-green umbrella and the towels laid out below it, I scan the horizon for my brother's orange surfboard. I find it, along with his mop of blond hair, sitting out beyond the break with two other figures I can tell are August and Zach.

"Are you coming out, or do you want to stay back and read?" Everett asks, slipping off his shirt. His arms are slowly being filled in with various tattoos August has given him over the last year, though his chest remains bare.

"I think I want to go out today." I don't surf often, but there is a blue board in the garage reserved for me. It hangs right between Leo's orange one and Everett's green one.

When it's just Leo, Everett, or Zach, I typically opt to stay on shore and read or write, or simply watch them. Leo, especially, is transcendent out there, and I never get tired of looking at him on the waves. When I surf with them, I mostly feel like I'm slowing them down. The only person somewhat capable of keeping up with Leo is Everett, and Leo needs his competition to keep himself fierce. Zach surfs like he's fighting the waves—he lives his entire life like he's fighting something, like it's an opponent he has to overcome.

It makes sense in the other sports he plays—football, basketball, baseball. What he fails to realize with surfing is that the water is your teammate, not your competitor. Zach doesn't understand that, and he moves aggressively through the water. It defeats the purpose of what surfing is supposed to be.

Surfing is simple for me. It has to be; it's the only way I can enjoy it. I don't have a competitive bone in my body, and I have no desire to be an expert or a champion at it. If I did, I would've lost interest long ago. The only person I want to compete with in my life is myself, and I think maybe that's why I like writing so much.

I can't put myself up against any other writer, because only I am capable of writing the story I want to tell. It's impossible for someone to create the exact same idea that exists inside my mind, and knowing that, whether it's good or bad, I'm still the only person in the world who can write the words flowing through my brain is comforting.

I love paddling beyond the break, love the movement of the ocean beneath my board, the wind in my hair when I glide through the water, but that's where it ends for me. The only person who seems to understand the way I feel about it—as something freeing and relaxing and easy—is August. So, I only like to surf when he's out there, too.

I shimmy out of my clothes and down to the bikini I'm wearing beneath them. I toss my hair into a loose bun atop my head before Everett and I zip up each other's wetsuits and head toward the waves.

I carry my board until I'm about hip-deep in the water, as it rises and crests against my thighs. My brother saddles up beside me, nodding before we both lie down and begin paddling toward the rest of our crew. It's sunny today, but the water's still cold since it's so early in the season. It's particularly windy too, whipping at my face and causing me to work twice as hard to make it past the break. Most days, the morning is the best time to surf; once the wind picks up, the waves turn choppy, which is both dangerous and annoying. Fortunately, I don't plan on doing much of anything besides floating today anyway.

I watch Leo paddle toward a swell creeping up in front of us. He pops up as it begins to crest, and just as I reach Zach, Leo swarms past me, riding it out.

"Hey, baby," Zach says, grabbing the front of my board and pulling me toward him. "What're you doing out here?"

Everett's already ahead of me, looking to catch the next suitable swell.

"Thought I'd come hang out today."

He smiles, soft brown eyes squinting in the afternoon sun as he reaches across our boards and grabs the nape of my neck, tugging me into him. "You look so fucking hot on a board." He kisses me hard, causing my heart to crash against my ribs like the whitecaps around us. "Wish you'd come out more often."

"Guess today is your lucky day," I respond breathlessly.

Zach pulls back, a soft smile on his face. He's in a good mood today. He loves me today.

Not every day is like this. In fact, most days aren't, especially in the year since he graduated high school. He's distant, and we're secretive. He's insecure about the fact that he still lives at home, his closest friends still in school. He has been working for a temp agency, mostly doing manual labor jobs around the area while he figures himself out.

If I thought I was Zach Hayes' dirty little secret before, that was nothing in comparison to how this last year has felt for us. Every other week, we're reduced to shouting voices and choking on tears. I'm begging him for something more, he's telling me I expect too much. We don't speak for long periods of time, only to realize we're so goddamn used to each other's touch, we're not sure how to cope without it, and he ends up in my bed or I end up in his.

Rinse and repeat.

I know the only way I'm ever going to move on is to quit

him cold turkey, but so long as he's around my brothers and living in my town, I can't let him go. He's too familiar, a battle I've been fighting for what feels like my whole life, and when I lay down my weapons, I can't remember who I am without them. Without him.

It's a toxic, raging, explosive kind of love. It's fierce, but it's fatal, and I know I'm not supposed to live my whole life like this. Just because it's the only love I've ever experienced doesn't mean it's the love that's worth the battle, but there are small slivers of me refusing to give up hope. Until those pieces of me can face the fact that this love is terminal, I can't break this cycle with him.

But today is a good day, at least.

Zach smiles at me in a way that makes my chest seize and my stomach hurt, like my body can't decide if it wants to lean into him and kiss him again or run away and spare my soul. I do the former. I always do the fucking former.

"I'm going to go chase down your brothers and kick their asses," he says as he pulls away.

"Good luck with that." I wink.

He rolls his eyes, as if he wants me to actually entertain the idea that he's a better surfer than Leo, and it only makes me laugh, turning his eye roll from something playful into something serious.

He lightly pushes my board back from his as he lies on his stomach and paddles out to where my brothers sit about twenty yards ahead. I glance sideways, where August straddles his board a few feet from me, his eyes firmly planted on the horizon.

He doesn't like to hang around Zach and me. Zach says it's because August is into me, which I disagree with. I know August finds me attractive, and hell, I find him attractive too.

He's probably the most beautiful person I've ever met, honestly. But it's more than that—we're best friends, and neither of us would ever allow a mere attraction to get in the way of that.

August doesn't like to hang around Zach and me for the same reason nobody else likes to hang around Zach and me: we're toxic. I'm sure he's tired of being put in the middle of his big brother and his best friend, feeling the pressure to choose a side when most of the time, we're both in the wrong.

I wouldn't want to hang around us either.

But now that Zach has paddled away, I turn my board and let myself drift toward August. It's not until mine bumps against his that he finally acknowledges me. His green eyes squint against the bright sun. "Hey."

"Hey, Augustus." I smile, my mind and bones and heart instantly settling.

Being around Zach is a thrill and a risk, and that's exciting, but there's something about knowing you're *safe* with another person that's freeing. I'm not going to accidentally say the wrong thing to set August off. He's never going to think I'm too dramatic, never going to be bored of my interests. I'm free to be myself in this moment with him, and for all the things Zach makes me feel, he doesn't make me feel that.

Chapter Ten

Elena

Age Twenty-One - October

"Tolerate It" - Taylor Swift

I watch the boats bob against the docks of the small harbor, floating above the evening fog so dense, I can't see the horizon line beyond the marina. It's eerie, unlike the picturesque Pacific Shores that bring people in from all over the world, but it's exactly the type of weather I've been craving after a long, hot summer.

Slipping my apron off my neck, I hang it on the hook behind the kitchen door before grabbing my purse, shouting a goodbye to the owner of Harbor Coffee, Jerry, and slipping out the front door. The bells on the handle knob chime as the cool sea air crashes against my face, and I take a deep breath of it.

Zach's crew won't dock for another half hour or so, but that gives me enough time to get home, shower, pop some ibuprofen because my period cramps are getting progressively worse, and watch his boat roll into the marina from my balcony while I sip on my evening cup of coffee.

It has been my favorite routine of ours lately.

Leo and I rent an apartment right on the harbor. It's about a two-minute walk from our front door to the coffee shop, and our third-floor balcony overlooks the marina, which means I have a near twenty-four-seven view of sailboats and fishing charters. My favorite part about living here, besides the view, is weekends, when I start my morning paddleboarding through the calm waters or writing on the docks.

The beach opposite the harbor has some of the best swells in the area, which is perfect for Leo when he's training at home and perfect for me because he's rarely home at all. He has been traveling the world almost constantly, surfing during competition season and modeling in the off-season. I'd fear him getting burnt out if I didn't know he was doing it all because he's constantly running away from something.

Running from the girl who ran from him.

Regardless, he makes a fuck ton of money, which means he pays our rent, and I get to live in a beautiful apartment mostly by myself.

The harbor is at the end of town, and while only blocks from our parents' house and the neighborhood we grew up in, it feels like its own environment, since we didn't spend much time down here as children. It feels like a little area that belongs to me, and I love it.

About six months ago, Zach began working on a crabbing rig. I know he doesn't love it, but it pays better than anything he has done before, and it lets him work out on the water, which I think he enjoys. I like it because I get to watch him come and go each day, and most evenings, he winds up in my bed.

I know he's lost right now. I know he struggles when he sees August and Leo following their dreams. I think he feels solidarity with Everett, who's a little lost too, though it's likely he'll take over our dad's garage when he's ready to retire. Everett, at least, has a path lined out for him.

That leaves me. I took one year of community college before realizing it wasn't the right fit for me, and I dropped out. I've never done well in a structured educational environment.

I've always preferred to learn on my own. I'm still working as a barista, and by all appearances, I'm as directionless as Zach.

Which makes me a little nervous about the conversation we're going to have tonight. I've been keeping a secret from him—from everyone except August—for years, and I've reached the point where I either need to give up on my own dreams or make them known to the entire world. I'm terrified for so many reasons, but a good chunk of them lie with how Zach is going to react.

We broke up for a solid six months just after I finished high school. Zach had moved out and was renting a house on the other side of town with friends. I was trying to attend college. He thought I spent too much time with August, and he felt he spent too much time with us *kids*, that he needed to grow up and get his shit together.

Which isn't entirely wrong, except none of us are the reason he's so fucking lost.

After distancing himself for a while and realizing the friends he was living with were a worse influence on him than all his younger friends, he came back around. I know he has always pressured himself to be the older, wiser, more mature, big-brother figure to Everett and Leo, but I think what he fails to understand is that they don't care what he does for work or whether he went to college. He is and always has been that to them.

I know they idolize him, and so does August. I imagine the pressure of that is intense, but I think it took Zach some soul searching to realize they're always going to look up to him no matter what he offers them, no matter how much money he makes, or what success looks like to him. For all the shit Zach has put me through, he has been a good friend to my brothers, and a good brother to his own.

After about a year of distance, he slowly came back to us. He started helping Leo train when he was in town, going out with Everett on the weekends. I know he helped August through his final year of high school by studying with him.

Throughout all of that, he kept his distance from me.

Until he began working in crabbing and we ran into each other on a few early mornings when he'd grab a coffee before his shift. Small talk turned into deep conversation, which turned into him showing up at my door one late night after work. Some kind of current runs between us, something that dims with distance, but when sparked by the smallest connection—a glance, a brush of his hand against mine, the sound of his laugh—it's like kindling. It takes very little to reignite our flame, and even less to have it blaze out of control, destroying everything around us.

I read enough to often find love compared to flame in the pages of my favorite romance novels. Burning, bright, warm. While all of that is beautiful, I think sometimes, we forget how destructive fire can be, how deeply a burn can scar, and how long it takes to recover when you've been turned to cinders.

Zach's love is fire. His flames turned me to ash, because I think I'm more like the Earth. I'm not meant to bear his destruction, yet despite it, I can't seem to snuff out those embers. When he's near, all it takes is one touch to reignite that spark, and suddenly, my world is erupting again.

The worst part of it all is that I love the burn.

I climb the stairs to the third floor of our building, letting myself inside the apartment. The first thing I do is search for something to help my cramps, but I come up short when—we're out of painkillers. *Fuck.* I sigh, stripping off my clothes and running into the kitchen to throw a kettle on the stove so I can at least brew some tea while I take a shower.

I ensure the water is extra hot as it pounds against my skin, quickly washing my face and hair. I get out and dry off before putting on my comfiest pair of sweats and my "Slut for Smut" crewneck—the one I'm no longer allowed to wear outside the house after a neighbor complained about me to my mother at the grocery store.

I heat up Rice Sock—Leo's appropriately named rice-filled sock, which he turned into a makeshift heating pad after mine exploded—in the microwave as I pour my tea, then make my way out to the balcony to settle in and wait for Zach. Our balcony is by far my favorite aspect of the apartment. The unit is spacious, with a large living room, two massive bedrooms, each with its own ensuite, a modern kitchen, and a formal dining room Leo has allowed me to repurpose as a workspace. The windows in that room overlook the harbor.

I decorated our balcony with plush loungers and ivy that crawls up the railing. Edison lights hang from the ceiling, and dark plum, black, and cream rugs and throw pillows accent the space. It's the perfect place to escape reality, which is exactly what I do as I settle in with the new thriller I've been dying to read.

A while later, I'm snapped out of the story by a distinct laugh ringing out in the distance. I stand, leaning over the railing. Zach is walking up the docks alongside a few of his crewmates. His head lifts, and a smile tugs at on his mouth when his eyes land on me.

"Fancy meetin' you here!" he calls out from below. "Gotta shower I can borrow? I smell like crab."

"That's just your natural musk," I snipe back, smirking at him.

His coworkers laugh, patting him on the back as they head through the dock gate and out into the parking lot. Zach shakes his head, shoulders bouncing with laughter. "Good thing you love my musk then, huh?"

I roll my eyes, knowing a blush is creeping up my cheeks as I step inside the apartment and shut the door behind me. A moment later, there's a knock at the front, and I pad across the linoleum floor and through the kitchen to throw the door open. Before I have a chance to greet him, Zach's shoving over the threshold and grasping my face, dragging his lips across my jaw and down my neck.

"What are you doing?" I damn near squeal. "I just showered!"

"Covering you in my musk, Elena." He laughs against my throat. "I have to mark my territory, so all the other fishermen know you're claimed."

"You're gross." I laugh, shoving him off me. "Go take a shower—I need to talk to you afterward."

Zach steps back, tilting his head at me. His brown eyes blaze with familiarity and allure—and also with curiosity and concern. "Good or bad?"

I smile, but it feels forced. "Good, I think."

His brows narrow, but he only nods as he begins to unbuckle his waders and kick off his boots before disappearing into my bedroom.

Fifteen minutes later, his hard footsteps pound down the hallway before he appears in the kitchen, opening my fridge and shuffling through its contents. Zach has on a pair of black joggers that hang low on his hips, revealing the cut V of his stomach that I love to run my tongue across.

I bite back a purr at the way his muscles flex as he reaches into my freezer and pulls out a box of taquitos. "Do you want any of these?" he asks, holding the box up.

"No." I shake my head, settling beneath my throw blanket

and grabbing my tea. "I have cramps, so I don't have much of an appetite."

He frowns, glancing at me cuddled up on the couch from the kitchen. "You should eat, baby. You're gonna feel worse with an empty stomach."

I shrug. "I'll eat in a bit."

"All right." He sighs, and a bout of butterflies spring up in my stomach at the concern in his voice. I know it's the bare fucking minimum, but when Zach shows any kind of care toward me, I can't help but feel like a sad puppy, desperate for an ounce of his affection.

He finishes heating up his food before he sits down next to me on the couch, kicking his feet up on the ottoman that doubles as a coffee table. The daylight is fading fast, darker than normal because of the dense fog. I reach up beside me, flicking on a lamp to cast the room in a soft, golden glow before tucking my legs underneath me and turning to face Zach.

"So...I've been working on something for a while, and I haven't been sure what I wanted to do with it when I finished, but I think I finally decided. I wanted to tell you about it and see what you think."

Zach's eyes go wide, and he chews his food slowly before setting his plate down on the ottoman. "What is it?"

"I wrote a book."

His brows shoot up, and his mouth scrunches to the side, as if to hold back laughter, instantly sending a flood of nerves to my stomach and an embarrassed flush to my face. My cheeks grow hot as he huffs a laugh and asks, "A book? What kind of book?"

I clear my throat awkwardly, looking around the room—anywhere but at him. "Well...you know I like romance and I like thrillers and...I like dark romance books that kind of mix the two together." I'm rambling, trying to explain myself. "I... I just had this idea of like...what if you took the villain—a killer—and what if they were actually just misunderstood the whole time? What if they also deserved a happy ending?"

I look at Zach again, and he raises an eyebrow, a smirk on his lips. "Are you serious? You wrote a romance book about a... serial killer?"

"Well..." I scratch my arm, restless with trepidation, suddenly anxious for his reaction. "She's more of a vigilante. She only targets men who've done terrible things. And the detective assigned to her case starts to unravel the mystery and the motive. He finds out all the horrible things these men have done, and then he starts to suspect her, the main character. As he investigates, gets to know her, he realizes she's not who he's made her out to be. They fall in love."

Zach's jaw drops open as he stares at me in shock. "But... she killed people? Like actually murdered people, and you're going to give her a happy ending? And what? Does she just keep killing people and the detective continues to cover it up?"

"Well...they kind of start killing people together, I guess? Kind of like a dark and twisted Bonnie and Clyde. They target the real villains of the world, and because he was a detective, he's always able to keep them one step ahead of the law, and that's what happily ever after looks like to them."

Zach laughs roughly, dragging a hand down his face. "That is insane, Elena. Absolutely insane."

"Oh," is my only response.

"Sorry. I didn't mean—" He shakes his head. "I knew you were into some morbid shit, but I had no idea it went that deep. I mean, you're using a pen name, right? If you publish this? *Do* you plan on publishing this?"

"I do." I nod, my breath hardly a whisper. "I planned

on publishing, and I hadn't thought much about the name I publish under."

"You have to use a pen name, Elena. I mean...I appreciate what you're doing here. I think it's cool, I do, but you've got to protect yourself." He leans forward, grabbing my hand. "How do you expect to keep a real job if *that* kind of book comes up every time someone searches you online? Do you really want your identity associated with that?"

That *kind of book*.

I rip my hand from his grasp. "I know there are benefits to using a pen name, but none of them have anything to do with my ability to maintain a *real* job." I hold up my fingers to make air quotes. "If I was ashamed of what I wrote, I wouldn't have written it. Of course I want to be associated with the art I created, Zach."

"You know what I mean, Elena. You can't let a hobby determine the rest of your life. You need to have a backup plan because the odds of you making any money—"

"First of all, I didn't do this to make money. I did it because I love stories and I love to write. Secondly, what is wrong with *wanting* to earn money from my passion? Why is it assumed I wouldn't?"

He tilts his head, giving me a deadpan expression. "C'mon, Elena. Do you know the percentage of authors who are able to make a full-time income from publishing their work? It's like... minuscule."

I roll my eyes, snorting. "Do you know what August said when I told him about this? When I explained my idea to him?" Zach's jaw ticks as his nostrils flare. "He told me he loved the way my brain works. He didn't tell me I was insane and ask me what kind of mask I planned to hide behind when I shared my art with the rest of the world."

Zach swallows, and I watch my words land, knowing exactly what would hurt him most. "You told my brother before you told me?"

I nod.

"Has he read it?"

I nod again.

"How long has he known?"

"Since I decided I wanted to write a book at all."

His gaze narrows. "And that was?"

"Eleventh grade." Around four years ago. I've written multiple stories in that time frame, but never anything I felt was worth sharing with the world, not until this one popped into my brain a few months ago and flowed from my fingertips like water.

Real hurt flashes across Zach's eyes, but he covers it quickly, dropping a bomb of his own. "My brother doesn't mean half the shit he says to you, Elena. He'll tell you whatever he thinks you want to hear because he wants to fuck you."

Those words are like a sucker punch to my stomach, the force of it rising into my throat, exiting my mouth in a choked laugh. "That's not—"

"Please," he scoffs. "August is in love with you." He gives me an unconvincing smile. "And before you get too excited about that, just remember—the only reason my brother wants you so bad is because you're in love with me. He's always pining after what's mine."

"You speak of me like I'm a toy you don't want to share."

Zach only shrugs.

My jaw trembles, my eyes ache with tears, but I refuse to let them fall. "So, August is in love with me, and I'm in love with you." My voice breaks. "Who're you in love with, Zach?"

He has never said those words to me, not in the nearly

ten years I've been chasing after him. Sometimes, I think that's exactly why I can't let go, why he won't say it. He doesn't want to give himself to me, not entirely, not the way I have to him. It's the piece of armor he keeps firmly over his heart, even when I've laid mine completely bare.

He loves me. He's not *in love* with me.

"You know how I feel about you, Elena. Don't weaponize that."

I tilt my head, forcing innocence into my voice as I ask, "You mean the way you weaponize my dreams just because you're insecure about not having any of your own?"

The words leave my mouth before I fully register them, and as I watch his face crumble, my hand falls over my mouth. I didn't mean to say that. I didn't mean to call attention to the thing I know brings him the most hardship. I didn't intend to speak the truth we both know too well but never address.

"I'm sorry, I—"

"You know what?" Zach pushes up from his knees, standing from the couch. "You're probably right, and you don't need me around to bring you down."

I can't muster a response, those tears I tried so hard to hide finally stream down my cheeks as he walks into my room and returns a moment later with his clothes, tossing on an old T-shirt.

That springs me into action. I jump up from the couch, a wave of nausea slamming into me. I can't tell if it's from my cramping or from the sight of him leaving. Zach is like a constant mirage I can't quite grasp, and every time he walks out a door, I feel sick with fear it's the last time I'll ever watch it happen.

"Zach, wait. Please don't. I—"

He grips the door handle, turning to face me once more.

"For what it's worth, I was only looking out for you. I'm sorry I don't have my shit together, and I wish you the best with publishing your book. I'm sure it's great."

My heart is in my throat, fear wrapping around it and pulling tight. I can't breathe, can't respond, can't think as I watch him walk out of my house and slam the door behind him.

My heart sinks, and I fight the urge to fall to my knees right in the entryway. The scene is so familiar, yet no less gutting as the slam of the door bounces off the walls of my chest cavity, fear grating against my ribs. Every interaction with Zach Hayes feels a little like walking on eggshells—constantly on edge, afraid I'll do or say the wrong thing and set him off. When we fight, my instinct is to find anything I can use as armor, any weapon to protect myself, because I know nothing slices me quite so deep as his harsh words and disappointed sighs.

Sometimes, I'm so desperate to get the last word, the last hit, the last swing of my sword, that I go too far. Zach and I spar with each other, we trade blows to the soul, but he always comes out on top, like an unwritten deal between us.

He chooses me because nobody else ever would. He tolerates things another man would've walked away from long ago. In return, I always let him win. He's always on top and in control. He always has the last word, and I'm always the one being reminded how lucky I am to have his attention.

So when I push a little too far, when I say something too real, something he can't come back from, he walks away. Sometimes for hours, sometimes for weeks, months.

And it's always my fault.

Rolling nausea presses against my abdomen, followed by a sharp, stabbing pain. My knees damn near buckle, and I turn, groaning as I waddle back to the couch and fall onto it. My breathing is labored and short, panting through my tears, heartache, and mother nature being a fucking bitch.

Without much thought, I grab my phone off the ottoman and dial the first number that comes to mind. I don't ask for favors often, and I certainly don't vent out my feelings or let others see me cry, but this instance calls for emergency help.

"Elena?" August's soft, gruff voice filters through my phone a moment later.

"Hi." I clear my throat, trying to rid the emotion from my voice. "Are you home?"

August has been living in San Diego for the last year, working as an apprentice for a tattoo artist and earning his two-year degree in Business Management. I don't see him nearly as often as I'd like, but he still comes home to stay with his parents in Pacific Shores most weekends. He normally doesn't make the drive until Friday, and today is Thursday, but I called on the off chance he might've driven up early.

"I'm still in San Diego. I'm heading home after work tomorrow," he says. "Why? And why are you crying?"

I sigh, realizing he's probably the only person on the planet who can tell when I'm upset, no matter how well I hide it. "I just...have bad cramps, and we don't have any ibuprofen. I don't feel up to driving to the pharmacy, so I was going to see if—"

"I'll be there in thirty."

"No, it's okay. You don't need to drive all this—"

"Elena," August says sternly. "I will be there in thirty minutes. Do you need anything besides ibuprofen? Tea? Snacks? You want me to pick you up an animal-style grilled cheese?"

Fuck. That sounds good.

"Umm..."

He chuckles. "Okay, give me thirty-five minutes then. You put on *Vanderpump Rules* and get Rice Sock ready. I've got Oreos and sweet pickles here I'll bring." My favorite snacks to eat when I'm writing. He's the only person who knows that about me. "I'll grab some burgers and some meds and be there soon, okay?"

"But you have to work tomorrow," I sniffle. My tears are free-falling again; it's moments like this when I miss my best friend, and I hate how rarely I get to see him nowadays.

"I don't work until ten. I'll crash in Leo's room tonight and drive back down early."

"Thank you," I breathe. "I love you."

"I love you, too, Elena." I can hear his smile before the line goes dead.

Chapter Eleven

August

Age Twenty - October

"the 1" - Taylor Swift

"Feeling better?" I ask as she lays her head against my chest.

We've watched almost an entire season of *Vanderpump Rules* in one sitting, and I think at least half my brain cells are dead. Elena was clearly upset and in pain when I arrived a few hours ago. She said she wasn't feeling well, and she has always had rough periods, but I couldn't help but feel like there was something more to it.

"Yeah." She nods against me sleepily. "Do you want to sit outside for a few before we go to bed?" She throws the blanket off our legs, padding over to the television stand and opening one of the drawers beneath it. She pulls out her bong, lighter, and a small bag of weed.

Everett broke the last bong Elena had, so for her birthday a few months ago, I bought her a plain glass one and hand-painted it with stars and constellations.

I'm not as big a smoker as the rest of them, but I imagine it does wonders for her cramps, so I get up and follow her out onto the balcony.

She silently loads her bowl, lights up, and takes a rip before handing it to me. As she exhales, puffs of smoke clouding the air around us, she says, "The fog cleared up, and you can actually see the stars tonight."

As I take a hit, I look out beyond her balcony. Boats softly rock in the water below us, and the eastern mountains cast a faint outline in the distance, the sky above them dotted with stars.

"It's beautiful," I say, knowing that, regardless of what view is in front of me, when Elena is beside me, she's all I'm going to see anyway.

"Do you think I should use a pen name when I publish?" she asks abruptly. I pass the bong back to her, turning to face her as I do. Her eyes are bright in the darkness.

"Yeah." I watch her face fall before I continue, "You've done something special, Elena. You're going to reach people with your words. I don't think it's a bad idea to protect yourself from the spotlight I have no doubt is about to be shining down on you."

Her crestfallen expression turns blindingly bright as a smile takes over her face. "Really?"

"Yeah." I smile back. "Your words are magic, but I also know you like your space and your privacy. You should give yourself the option to protect that. Doesn't mean you're hiding yourself or that what you've written is anything you need to hide from."

She nods. "You don't think writing is going to ruin my chances of finding a real job?"

"What is a real job?" I laugh. "No. I don't think it's going to hurt your ability to do anything, Elena. And honestly, I read a lot of damn books. You were born to be a writer. You're going to go far with this."

She sighs, taking another hit. On her exhale, she says, "I feel like nobody understands me except you."

"I feel like that too," I respond. "Did my brother say something?"

I know she decided recently to go through with self-publishing the book she has been working on the last few months. She recently sent her manuscript to a freelance editor she found online and is doing the preparation of getting it ready to release. She was mentally preparing herself to tell her parents, brothers, and Zach. Now, I'm wondering if that's exactly what she tried to do tonight.

"He told me I was insane."

My jaw tightens at that. "Well, he hasn't fucking read it, so his opinion really should be inconsequential."

She nods. "I know. It's just...he seemed almost embarrassed? Like he encouraged me to use a pen name, and I think it was because he's afraid to be associated with someone who writes what I do."

I watch her—her beautiful face deep in thought as she stares up at the stars. "Have you ever thought that maybe it isn't him?"

"I know it's not him." She doesn't look at me, her eyes instead tracing the constellations above us. "Love isn't supposed to feel like this. But I've spent all my life wanting so desperately for him to be *the one*. I don't think I know how to let go of that yet."

I swallow down all the words I can't say. I stretch my hand across the couch between us, her fingers brush against mine. I dig into the fabric, desperate to hold her instead but knowing I can't. Unsure if I'll ever be able to. Terrified she'll never stop belonging to someone else.

She's still looking at the sky, lost in space, as always. I'm still staring at her, lost in her eyes, like always.

"Well, for the sake of whoever *the one* is, I hope you figure it out soon. I know somebody's out there waiting to give you everything you've ever wanted."

Her head snaps sideways, eyes meeting mine. Her brow furrows, and I want so desperately to know what's going through her mind right now, but I'm too terrified to ask. She opens her mouth before clamping it closed, like whatever she was about to say, she thought better of.

"Let's go to bed."

I nod wordlessly, following her back inside. We walk down the hallway past the kitchen to where the two bedrooms sit across from each other. I turn toward Leo's door and she turns toward her own, stopping suddenly on the threshold.

"Augustus," she whispers, turning to face me. An unreadable expression envelops her face, sending my heart into a spiral—I have no idea what she's about to say next. "Do you want to have sex with me?"

My heart, my soul, all the contents of my stomach leap into my fucking throat. My cock jumps right alongside them, and I'm stuck floundering in the hallway, mouth opening and closing as my mind attempts to come up with a response.

"Ar–are you offering?" I manage to ask.

You fucking idiot.

Thankfully, she only laughs. "No. I just... Are you attracted to me in that way?"

"Every person on this goddamn planet is attracted to you in that way, Elena. Trust me." Her eyes go wide, and if I'm not mistaken, I think her pupils might dilate. "But you're my best friend, and that comes first to me. I wouldn't risk it for a one-time thing. Plus, you've never been apart from my brother long enough for me to attempt to make it more than that."

I may have laid myself too bare with that response, exposed too much of the truth I've spent half my life keeping to myself.

In fact, I know I've said too much when Elena's breath catches, and she takes a step back, like the words were a physical hit.

I watch her throat bob as she swallows, shaking away whatever thoughts are plaguing her mind. "Right." She licks her lips, eyes tracking my body head-to-toe, and suddenly, I realize it might be a very bad idea for me to sleep here tonight. If she gives me the green light, I'm taking it, my brother be damned. "Well, I hope I find *the one* someday soon, too."

She doesn't move right away, and neither do I. We stare each other down, the tension growing thick and hot between us. She looks at me like she wants me to say something—do something—and I know I'm looking at her the same.

I can't be the one to make that move, though. If she's going to choose me, I need to hear the words. I need to know it's me, not him. I need to know it'll never be him again, and until she figures that out, I won't let this happen between us.

"Goodnight, Elena," I say, stepping into Leo's bedroom. I don't give myself the chance to watch the expression on her face as I shut the door behind me.

Chapter Twelve

Elena

Age Twenty-Three - February

"i'm worried it will always be you" - Katie Gregson-MacLeod

"Ad Elena, la mia ragazza perfetta. Non potrei essere più orgogliosa di essere tua madre." My mom raises her glass, and everyone politely blinks at her because they don't have a damn clue what she's saying. However, *I* know she's proud of how far her Italian has come in the last few years.

"She said Elena's her favorite child and we should all raise our glasses." Everett smiles, lifting his beer from the center of the table.

My mother rolls her eyes but doesn't bother correcting him as everyone lifts their cups, congratulating me. My parents, both brothers, August, Zach, and their parents, plus a couple of my coworkers from Harbor Coffee, are here. We rented out the upper deck patio at the Seaside Sunset on the pier, the sun sinking over the Pacific behind us as we celebrate my publishing deal.

I released my first book last year, and it did a lot better than I ever imagined it would. I landed an agent about six months ago and spit out two more books in this same series. My agent pitched them to traditional publishing houses, and a few weeks ago, we received an incredible deal: the three books I've already written, plus three more I've got planned out within the same series. The advance allowed me to quit my job at the coffee shop and pursue writing full time. I might have deadlines, a book tour, and an entire team of people putting pressure on me now, but it's more than worth it to have this be my whole life.

I take a sip from my drink, meeting August's eyes across the table. His smile is wide and genuine, emerald eyes sparkling as he mouths, *I'm so proud of you.* Emotion pricks in my eyes; none of this seems real right now, and I know more than anyone else, I wouldn't have made it here without him.

There is a pressure on my thigh, and I glance down to find Zach's massive hand splayed against my leg, squeezing gently. I look up at him, and he's smiling too, though it doesn't appear quite as genuine. I force a smile back. My writing's been a sore spot between us these last couple of years. Zach continues to bounce around from job to job, and I know he's still resentful of my success, but at the very least, he doesn't say anything negative about it anymore.

"So, Elena—how did you come up with the name Violet Rose?" Sadie, August and Zach's mother, asks me from the other end of the table.

"Oh." My eyes meet August's, and Zach squeezes my thigh again. "Well, Rose is my middle name, so that made sense. I almost used my real first name, but I decided to go with Violet instead. I thought two flowers as a name flowed well together."

Violet was actually August's idea. He came up with it when he was tattooing the flowers along my forearm last year. I'd finally convinced him when I graduated high school to get a matching tattoo with me. It started with constellations. Mine is behind my ear: Libra, his sun sign. He has a Leo constellation on his wrist for me.

It wasn't until last year that I convinced him to do

something more detailed, and that's how I ended up with wild violets dotted between my wrist and my elbow, along with matching vines and leaves. The same flowers he used to draw on my skin with pen, that he picked for my birthday every year. Those flowers belong to us. It's another secret of ours, so choosing that name was my way of thanking him for all his support.

"I love the sentiment behind it." Sadie smiles, but like her oldest son's, it's unconvincing. She has never liked me. She thought I was a bad influence on August when we were younger, and she convinced herself I corrupted Zach's purity by taking his virginity. That thought always makes me laugh, as if he wasn't a seventeen-year-old boy with raging fucking hormones.

I know she especially doesn't like the content of the literature I write, but I couldn't care less about her opinion, honestly. She's a washed-up soap actress everyone forgot about twenty years ago.

"Thank you," I say, forcing kindness into my voice.

Zach leans into me. "You're coming home with me tonight, right?"

He doesn't sound seductive and smooth like he normally does when he's propositioning me like this. No, his voice sounds tight and distant, like he's not fully invested. Still, I nod all the same, because I seem to be physically incapable of turning him down.

Zach lightly kisses me behind the ear, right over the tattoo his brother put there. As his lips touch my skin, I lift my eyes, gaze clashing with August's. He watches the gesture, and an unmistakably painful expression washes over his features before he turns his head and looks away.

Suddenly, my appetite is gone.

"Did you enjoy dinner?" Zach asks as he shuts the door to his small studio apartment and we both kick off our shoes.

"Yeah." Tension hangs thick in the room, and every part of me feels on edge. "Did you?" I ask, turning to face him as I awkwardly sit on the edge of his bed.

He shrugs. "Wasn't my party."

I tilt my head, attempting to read his face—and failing, just as I always have. Deciding to go ahead and address whatever weirdness is floating between us, I say, "You don't seem happy for me."

He slowly closes his eyes, as if preparing himself for what's about to come. "That's not it, Elena."

"Want to tell me what *it* is, then?"

He lets out a long sigh, leaning back against the kitchen counter, like he's trying to keep as much space between us as possible. "I want kids."

What the fuck. "Umm..."

He shakes his head, dragging a hand down his face. "I don't mean right now. I mean in general."

"With me?" The question comes out apprehensively.

I definitely don't want kids. Not right now, and probably not ever.

"I don't know." He pushes off the counter and takes a step forward. "And isn't that a problem? I mean, it's been a decade of this back and forth. I should know by now, shouldn't I?"

All my internal organs feel like they're about to fall out of my ass. "We're still young," I murmur.

"Yeah, but I want to settle down soon. I want to get married. I want to have kids and own a home. I want to make a life, and you're just starting your career. You have so much ahead of you." He closes the distance between us, taking my face between his hands. "I'm so excited for you. For that. But I... I don't think it's something I signed up for, Elena. I don't think we make sense anymore."

"We've never made sense, Zach." My chest feels hollow, but my throat feels stuffed. My nose stings as it attempts to hold the pain behind my eyes. "That hasn't stopped us before."

"We were kids."

My jaw strains, lips trembling as I fight to halt my tears. I close my eyes—fighting a war to maintain my composure. Zach has broken up with me a million times, but this is the realest it has ever been. Because he's right. We've reached the point in our lives where our decisions have harsher consequences. Time starts to move faster, and infatuation isn't enough anymore.

"I wish you would've figured this out before you made me fall in love with you," I whisper.

"I didn't make you do anything, Elena. I didn't ask you to fall in love with me, and you didn't ask me if I wanted to run alongside you when you decided to chase your dreams." His touch is soft where his words are sharp, as if he's shoving a blade through the center of my chest and then asking me why I'm bleeding all over his clothes. "I think maybe we should just end—"

"No." My brain didn't give my mouth permission to say the word, but somehow, it floats in the air between us anyway. I grip Zach's forearms, pushing him back. He lets me flip us so he's sitting on the bed, and I'm crawling atop him. "Please don't say that. Don't do this," I beg, moving his arms to my waist and dragging my hands up his chest, burrowing my face in his neck.

I don't know why I'm doing this right now, delaying the inevitable, but I can't stop myself. His scent is too familiar, his touch too well known. He's all I've ever had, and I physically don't know how to get up and walk away from it—even when I'm certain I should. We're heading toward disaster; I can see it on the horizon, but I've spent my entire life trying to make this love work. To throw that all away would deem it worthless.

The pain, the tears, the fights, all of it for nothing.

No epic love story, no happily ever after.

Desperation swallows me whole as I grind against Zach's lap, wanting—needing—him to feel my anguish. If I can't do anything else, I can remind him of our chemistry, the burning desire between us that we can't ever seem to snuff out, no matter how hard we try.

"One more night," I plead, kissing his neck. "Please."

"Elena." My name leaves his lips like a curse.

"I need you," I cry against his jaw. "I need you. I don't care about the rest of it."

He pauses, pulling back to meet my eyes. Swiping a thumb beneath my cheek and taking my tears with it, he drops his forehead against mine. "Why can't I let you go?" he whispers, voice breaking with torment.

"I don't know." Our heartbeats pound together, rough and dangerous and broken.

He swallows, hand snaking behind my head, grip tightening in my hair. No words left to be said, he hauls his mouth to mine, cementing our descent into the madness of each other's souls.

Chapter Thirteen

Elena

Age Twenty-Four - September

"History Of Man" - Maisie Peters

"I got a job in Wyoming, and I leave on Sunday."

The words ring through my skull, ricocheting off the corners of my brain, but I can't make sense of them. Sure, months ago Zach told me we needed to end things because he didn't want to chase my dreams with me, and I didn't want to have his babies, but after that night, we never spoke of it again. He continued working various temp jobs; I got published, did my book tour, and settled into my life as a full-time author.

He didn't ask me about my writing, and I didn't ask him where we stood. For the first time in our lives together, we were uncomplicated.

Until now.

"What's in Wyoming?" Despair funnels itself into the depths of my body as I stare him down.

"I'm going to work on a cattle ranch, for a year to start, and see if I like it."

"Doing what?" My tone comes out cold and snappy.

"Whatever they tell me to."

My teeth clench hard enough to crack, jaw trembling beneath the weight of what he'd just dropped on me. "And that's better than being here? With your friends and family?

With me?"

"You mean the friends who are traveling the world? Or opening their own businesses? Or my parents, who just bought their second home in Palm Springs and are hardly ever in town? Or how about you, Elena? Your deadlines where you shut yourself inside your office for weeks at a time? Your book tours and signing events on the weekends? I never see you either."

Because you never come around.

I know it's hard for him to watch everyone else succeed when he feels he's failing himself, but if he gave me a chance, I'd make time for him. I've always made time for him.

"Everyone is surpassing me, and I'm the oldest." He slaps his chest. "I'm the big brother. I'm the one who's supposed to have it figured out, the one they look up to, and I'm a fucking mess. I'm lost. I have no clue what I'm doing or which direction I'm going in. I need a change."

"So you're just going to leave? No notice? No warning? Is this supposed to be your goodbye?"

Zach texted me an hour ago asking if he could come over and talk. Prior to that, I hadn't seen him for three days, but the last morning we spent together was wrapped up in my bed. This was the last thing I could've expected to happen.

He grabs my hands, offering no other explanation than, "I'm sorry," before standing and heading toward the front door.

"I won't wait for you," I whisper, more to myself than to him.

To my surprise, he laughs. *Laughs.* "Okay, Elena."

I stand, spinning to face him. "You don't believe me, do you? You want to pack up and leave without notice, move across the country, go off grid, and leave me sitting right here, waiting to welcome you home with open arms when you show your face again a year later?"

He's staring at me blankly, zero emotion in his deep brown eyes. "I didn't say I wanted that."

"No. You just expect it."

He doesn't respond.

Now I'm the one laughing. "Because that's what I've always been to you, right? The girl you lie to, cheat on, use like a toy. You leave when you get bored, and every time you come back, I'm right where you left me."

Zach's nostrils flare, eyes on fire. "That's all you fucking care about? Really? I just spilled my fucking guts to you, and your only concern is how it makes *you* feel?"

"I empathize with you—really, I do!" I shout. "But there are a million different ways you could've gone about this, chief among them, *communicating* with me. Springing this on me two days before you plan to fucking leave is cruel. We've been together for a decade, Zach. You owed me more."

My voice breaks on those final words, and I watch Zach's face shudder at the sound, the only evidence he's aware of how much he's hurting me right now. That he's hurting too. "I don't owe you anything, Elena."

Those words split me open, and the expression on his face digs the hole he'll bury me in.

"Then I don't owe you anything either. You walk out right now, and this is done. For good." My vision blurs through the mess of my tears, and I realize—I won't even get to see him clearly when he shuts that door on me.

"I know," he whispers, grabbing the handle.

"Are you threatened by it?" I ask, voice a desperate plea. His brows shoot up in question. "The way you love me. The power I hold over you because of it," I continue, grasping for any excuse to prolong this moment. Of making him stay. "Or were you never in love with me to begin with?"

Zach shakes his head, and I imagine how I look right now: a broken girl with stars in her eyes, begging for the only thing she ever truly wanted from him.

"You know how I love you."

"I asked if you were *in* love with me."

There's genuine pain on his face when his gaze meets mine, burning into my soul for the final time, leaving it branded and bleeding. "I can't give you the answer you want to hear."

My eyes fall closed, unwilling to watch this ending. For the first time, he doesn't slam the door when he leaves. The click of it falling into place is gentle and soft, echoing through the chamber of my chest like the hammering of a final nail in my coffin.

Chapter Fourteen

August

Age Twenty-Three - January

"Violets for Roses" - Lana Del Rey

"What're you drawing?"

I startle, jumping at the sound of her voice. I turn, finding Elena standing behind me, the golden sun casting a glow on her face. "What are you doing here?"

"Stalked your location." She shrugs, sitting down beside me. "I hit my word count goal for the day, cleaned my entire apartment, and didn't want to be alone, so I decided to come find you."

I chuckle, turning back to my sketchbook. "Glad you did."

"This is your first time out of the shop in forever, it feels."

I nod. "We had to cut the power for the day so they could do some installation, and when it started to get dark, there was no way I could continue working with only flashlights, so I came out here to watch the rest of the sunset."

I've been working with Jensen, the artist I had my apprenticeship with, for the last two years. He offered me a job after I got my license, and while I preferred living in Pacific Shores, I couldn't turn down the job.

Until last year, when Leo bought out the entirety of the Pacific Shores Boardwalk. The small businesses we loved as kids have slowly gone under over the years, one by one. With the money he made from surfing and modeling, Leo reinvested in the community by buying the entire building, all five suites that line the promenade in front of the pier.

He and Everett plan on opening a surf shop in the first unit, and they offered me a space as well. A tattoo and piercing parlor. I chose the suite on the far end, opposite the surf shop, so it would feel like my own space. Everett, Leo, and I have been working our asses off the last few months to get everything refurbished and ready for business. It's exhausting, but we're getting close to opening, and I couldn't be more excited.

"You think of a name for it yet?" Elena asks, plopping down beside me.

"Nope," I lie. I definitely have a name picked out, but I'm not ready to tell her yet.

The sun sinks low over the Pacific, casting the sky in cotton candy colors, the ocean below us in gold.

Elena hums. "Well, what are you drawing?"

"Just playing around with some sketches." I flip my book closed before she can see what I'm actually working on.

She sighs, laying her head against my shoulder, watching the sky fade. "Draw something that reminds you of me."

I smile to myself. She asks me to do that all the time, and I always draw the same thing. She must have enough sketches of violets to line her entire apartment, but every time I make her something new, her face lights up like it's the first time she has ever seen it.

"What've you been working on?" I ask as I get to work. We've both been so busy lately, I haven't had time to talk to her much about her new manuscript. It's the fifth book in her ongoing series, all surrounding domestic villains and how they overcome their darkness through love and romance. Her writing is poetic and soft, though the content of her stories is dark and morbid. The combination of it all creates a unique experience readers can't get enough of.

I was the first person to read her work, and it still feels like an honor, the same way all those poems she used to write, that I still keep beside my bed, feel like a privilege. People all around the world pay for her words now, and I've always had them for free.

Elena lies down on the grass, putting her head in my lap. Her flawless face is incredibly distracting, and every time our eyes meet, she smiles at me in a way that makes it hard to breathe.

Rambling about her manuscript, she tells me every detail, and before long, the sun has completely disappeared, and it's too dark for me to keep drawing. I set my sketchbook beside us, leaning back on my elbows.

"I'm trying really hard to be happy," she says softly after we've finished talking.

"You miss him?" I ask.

Zach left three months ago to work on a ranch in Wyoming. There's no cell service out there, so he's only able to call on Sundays, when the workers head into town. I know he's purposely keeping his distance from Elena, but he has been checking in with me, our friends, and my parents. He seems to be doing well—enjoying it, even. It's like whatever answers he was searching for out there, he's finally finding.

I don't tell Elena when I speak to my brother, I don't want to upset her. I've also found that when I'm keeping my relationships with Zach and Elena completely separate, I like him a lot more. He has always been a great brother, a good friend—he's just a shitty boyfriend, and when he's being that to the woman I'm also in love with, it cuts deeper.

"I don't want to, but I do." She sits up, dark curls flowing wildly around her face as she spins toward me, crossing her legs. "I think I need to...date? Maybe? I need to remind myself how much better off I am. Zach, he..." She sighs. "He didn't want me to be me. He didn't like what I read or what I wrote. He thought I was annoying when I talked about the stars, and he didn't like the idea of my body being covered in tattoos. He never wore the necklaces I made him. He didn't believe me when I told him citrine brought prosperity and meditating with certain crystals could manifest the path he was so desperate to find." She rolls her eyes, but I smile. I love when she rambles about the things she's passionate about. "My point is—now that he's gone, I've remembered who the fuck I am. I'm dark and weird and moody and stubborn. Zach wanted me to fit inside a certain box, be the type of girl who belonged on the arm of the all-American boy next door like him, and I've never been that girl." Her face drops into a frown. "I think that's why he was never fully able to show us off to the world, to give us a title. He was always a little embarrassed of me."

"There is nothing about you to be embarrassed by, Elena." I lean forward, grasping her chin and lifting it, forcing her eyes to meet mine, forcing her to see the fervor in my face when I say those words.

She smiles softly. "I know. It felt like Zach wanted me to be..." Her brow furrows with deep thought, eyes darting to the sketchbook sprawled in the grass beside me. "He wanted me to be roses, but I'm not." Elena's gaze meets mine. "I'm a violet."

"Violets are my favorite."

"That's because you're a violet too." She laughs, shoving my shoulder. "I guess I just kind of feel like there is this film covering my body, the sheet he tried to hide me behind. I want to rip it off, cleanse myself of it." She shrugs, a small smile accenting her lips. "And they say the best way to get over someone is to get under—"

"No." The word rips from my throat, far more aggressively than I intend, but the second I realized the direction her thoughts were going, I cut in.

I don't often let my thoughts filter to the possibilities of Elena being with another man, because that man had always been my brother. I'd always assumed if it wasn't him, it'd be me, and realizing she could end up with someone else entirely is a sickness I feel down to my marrow.

My tone is harsh enough that Elena rears back, eyes going wide, then narrow.

"Sorry." I clear my throat. "I just..." I stop myself. I'm done hiding the truth. My brother isn't here for her to go running back to, and we're not kids anymore. "Actually, you know what?" I shake my head. "I'm going to be honest. I cannot stand the idea of hearing about you with another man again. I've dealt with it my entire fucking life, and I won't do it anymore. I won't watch you give yourself to anyone else."

Elena looks at me like she can't decide if she's pissed off, confused, or intrigued. "What do you propose then, Augustus?" she asks, voice dropping to a rasp. "That I become some kind of celib—"

"If you want to use someone to get over my brother..." I sit up on my knees, crawling toward her as she falls back onto the grass. Something akin to allure rages in her eyes as I hover over her. "Use me."

She licks her lips. Chills race down my body, settling in my core as she slides a hand up my back, cupping the nape of my neck—a featherlight touch we've never dared to share before.

"What do you mean by that, August?" she whispers.

"I mean..." I breathe, hardly able to think past the way she feels beneath me. "You need attention? I'll give you that.

You need to be reminded who you are? Creative? Captivating? Intelligent? Stubborn and beautiful and eccentric? I'll do that." I drop my head, and suddenly, I'm close enough to share the breath spilling out of her perfect mouth in short, rapid bursts. "You need someone willing and eager to cater to your every need, Elena? Because I've been dreaming about being that man my entire goddamn life."

Her eyes widen like chocolate saucers at my offering, and I'm free-falling into their depths, watching the stars above our heads glisten inside her irises.

"What about our friendship?" she asks.

"You're honestly going to tell me right now that you believe that's all I've ever seen you as?"

She bites her lip, gaze dropping, as if she's afraid to look at me. "He said it was a fleeting crush." Her eyes meet mine again. "Zach. He said you only wanted me because I was his, that you'd always wanted what was his. He said it was all surface level."

I swallow, lifting off her and sitting back on my heels. "I've always looked up to him. I still do." I wipe a hand down my face, a sudden pang of guilt hitting my chest, but one look at Elena's has it clearing just as quickly. "It felt like he had everything I didn't. But not you. You are not something I wanted *because* of him. I've wanted you all this time because you're...because you're my person."

Elena's expression softens. Shifting from heat and bewilderment to something more like awe and torment. "Why haven't you ever told me?"

I sigh, looking down at the grass, digging my fingers into the soil. "You saw him first."

"August," she begins, but I cut her off, needing her to hear the whole of it.

"The day I found you in my tree, filling your shirt with

flowers and rambling about books? I knew about thirty seconds into that conversation I was going to fall in love with you. I didn't realize you knew my brother until you walked away."

"You never said anything," she whispers.

"You smiled when I said his name." I shrug. "He's always been a flirt, charming as hell. I may have been eleven at the time, but even then, I knew the effect he had on people. You weren't the first girl to smile like that after falling for him, and I wasn't going to root for your broken heart, Elena." I lift my eyes, meeting her gaze. "Even if I wasn't the one holding it. I've only ever wanted your happiness."

Her big, brown eyes gloss over, but she doesn't let her tears fall. "I'm sorry." Bottom lip trembling, she closes the distance between us, scrambling onto my lap to straddle my hips. "I've been so blind." She takes my face between her hands, and the feel of her skin on mine is like a flame to frostbite, a stitch to a wound, ice to a burn. "You've always seen me with the utmost clarity."

"Elena," I whisper her name like a prayer, like she's the god I'm hoping will finally answer it. My hands slide up her thighs, warmth blooming beneath my palms as I grasp her waist and tug her against me. Our bodies align in a way that feels like coming home.

Her gaze focuses on my mouth as her nose skims mine, and my lips part, tasting her breath. Elena and I have always felt a little like the moon and the Earth. I orbit her, while she orbits something else entirely. But in this moment, as she cups my jaw and brings my mouth to hers, we're colliding. Gravity falls apart as we fall together, and for all the destruction we're about to create, kissing her feels cosmic.

Kismet.

Elena

"Ultraviolet" - Aiden Bissett

I inhale the tortured whimper as it leaves his lips, his mouth soft and delicate against my own. It doesn't feel real. It feels like more. It feels like how I imagine every moment in a story when someone kisses the right person for the first time.

It's not fire—it's Earth. It's nature. The cool rush of air against your face, the feel of flower petals on your fingertips, touching clouds, and looking at candy-colored skies.

I never knew it could feel this way.

His hands press against my back, slowly skating beneath the hem of my shirt and caressing my bare skin. It sends sensation up my spine, spreading soft warmth from my cheeks to my toes. Tentatively, he slips his tongue into my mouth, the taste of him like a dream I couldn't remember having but now feel I'll never be able to forget.

Another needy noise leaves his throat as I give him everything I have, moving my hips against his body, letting our tongues dance, our lips move in sync.

The kiss deepens, his hands in my hair, cradling my face like I'm something to cherish. I've never been touched like this before—like I'm delicate, too valuable to break. It's purposeful and fierce and consuming, but it's not chaotic or fleeting or harsh. It doesn't feel like craving pain; it feels like healing souls.

August's lips feel like they were always meant to be mine—not something I have to chase or something I have to run from. He kisses me like he's waited his whole life for it.

It's desperate. It's passionate. It's...real. So real, beyond words. My mind races my heart at the tenderness of his touch.

I can't comprehend how it feels so incredibly right; he has been here all this time, and I haven't seen him.

That truth begs me to kiss him deeper, to wrap my arms around his neck and press into him harder, merging our bodies until I can erase all the years of distance that never should've been there.

Because *this* is what I've been missing all this time.

What always should've been.

"Elena," he groans, saying my name like he has been blessed by it.

I pull back, my hands running rampant through his hair, twisting in the soft curls I've always loved so much. My face is still between his hands as I tilt his up to mine. His eyes are cascading shades of emerald, reflecting the glow of the night sky, matching the glimmer left by our kiss on his full lips.

His beautiful eyes fall closed, his hold on me tightening, like he's trying to grasp it before it disappears. "You have no idea how long I've waited for that." His words catch on a tortured breath.

"I hope I lived up to expectations." I laugh hoarsely, still lost in the feel of us.

He drops an arm to my waist, dragging me against him. "You are the embodiment of all my dreams, Elena." His mouth moves against my throat as he speaks, the words stitching themselves into the fabric of my soul.

He looks up as I look down, our lips a hairsbreadth apart. I close my eyes in anticipation, but August surprises me as he says, "I can't do that again until you're sure." He tucks a stray curl behind my ear. "I can't have your bits and pieces. Not these ones. I don't want your body if I can't have your heart too. I don't want your heart if I'm not the only one holding it." He swallows hard, like the words are thick, stuck inside his throat.

"I can't bear anything less."

I don't open my eyes, too afraid of what I'll find staring back at me if I do. Instead, I press my forehead against his. I want to tell him I'm ready to give him everything—but I know I can't make promises I won't keep. Not with August. He's too important, and whatever just happened between us is far too real. Our past, and the people in it, is far too complicated not to consider.

I nod, and he sighs against my lips.

"You were in love with me?" I find myself asking for—needing—the confirmation. Confirmation that someone could've ever yearned for me like that, because a small part of me has always wondered if it was me, if I was the problem, the reason he couldn't call it that.

My eyes are still closed as he pulls away, shuffling with movement before he nudges something sharp against my hand. When I open them, I drop my gaze to his sketchbook propped between us. I take it between my hands, slipping my thumb through the cover before lifting my eyes to search his for permission. He offers a shallow nod, and as I flip through the book, I find page after page of...me. In black and white, drawings of myself stretch across the canvas paper, images of me reading, laughing, even working—curled on my couch, brow furrowed in concentration with my computer on my lap.

For years, August and I have spent our days and nights in peaceful silence—me reading or writing, and him drawing. He's always been private about his pieces, but I never could've imagined he was spending his time studying me.

Shocked tears drip down my cheeks, emotion lodged inside my throat and rendering me speechless. I softly close the book, setting it on the ground beside us before surging forward and taking his face between my hands, pressing my lips to his. He said he wouldn't kiss me again, but I don't have words to express the feeling coursing through my veins, I can only attempt to show him.

"I've always been in love with you," August whispers, kissing away the moisture beneath my eyes.

I shiver as his words move through me, planting themselves inside my chest. For the first time in my life, I feel capable of being loved—I'd just been asking for it from the wrong person.

I open my eyes, taking in the sight of the man below me. I've always felt like he was the most beautiful person I'd ever known, but looking at him now, it all feels heightened.

"I think I could fall in love with you, too."

He smiles, but it doesn't reach his eyes. "Don't say that again until you're sure."

Chapter Fifteen

Elena

Age Twenty-Four - February

"Heavenly" - Cigarettes After Sex

Rain pelts the pavement as I jog across the street, its scent overpowering the smell of the ocean in a surprisingly pleasant way.

I run around the backside of the Boardwalk, careful not to catch the attention of my brothers through the window of their soon-to-be surf shop. I might stop in and check out their progress when I'm done, but speaking with August is my priority right now.

We haven't talked since we kissed in the dark two weeks ago. Since he told me he's in love with me. That he has always been in love with me.

I wanted to take more time to grieve my relationship with Zach, to consider what it would mean to take things with August to the next level. He has been my best friend my entire life, and I'm not sure who I would be if not for him, and regardless of anything else, I can't lose that. I also can't ignore the repercussions of jumping from the arms of one brother to another, but I was clear with Zach that I wouldn't wait for him, that I'd move on if he left.

Sure, moving on with his brother might make me kind of an asshole, but it's clear Zach has known the way August has felt about me all this time, and he continued keeping me on his hook anyway. He dangled me in front of his brother like I was something to show off, something to possess just because he could, even if he didn't really want me.

Knowing that should make me feel bitter. It should break my heart and make me rage, but it doesn't. Honestly, it just makes me feel tired—tired of wasting so much of my life, all of my energy, on someone who never truly saw me. All I want now is to turn that energy toward the one person who has always looked at me clearly, who never tried to change my colors or pluck my petals. The person who has loved me all along.

Since that kiss, I see it—see him—every time I close my eyes. I feel him when I touch my lips, when my hand slips between my legs in the middle of the night. I've always known I had an attraction to August, one I refused to explore, but now, it's like something inside me has been awakened, and I'm consumed by him entirely.

It was for the sake of our friendship, and both of our hearts, that I've stayed away the last two weeks, thinking and overthinking every scenario and outcome of the predicament we've found ourselves in. I've realized there is no part of me that doesn't want to take this risk and explore whatever has bloomed between us. There are only parts of me that know I'd regret it if I never tried.

The back door to the last suite on the Boardwalk is unlocked, and I slip inside quietly, wiping my feet on the welcome mat before following the narrow hallway that leads to the front of what will soon become his tattoo parlor.

The open space is nearly empty, save for a few tray tables, two benches, a chair, and a reception desk near the front. There isn't any art on the walls or decor up yet. There also isn't any August, though I was sure I saw his Bronco parked behind the building.

"Augustus?" I call out, turning slowly around the building.

A moment later, he comes around the corner I imagine leads to some kind of back office. His brows are furrowed beneath his glasses, and a smile blooms across his face when he realizes it's me. August leans against the wall, crossing his arms. My eyes rake up his body, starting at the worn Converse on his feet, his black jeans, the white T-shirt hanging off his slim, tall frame, tight over his toned, tattooed arms.

He's smirking at me now as he realizes I was checking him out, and I don't even care because *goddamn*, he's hot as hell.

"Hi," he says.

"Hi," I respond, suddenly out of breath. I inhale deeply, willing confidence as I prepare myself for what I have planned. I'm about to ask for something I've honestly wanted for a while, something I've always known I'd only trust August to do, but the meaning behind it is completely different now. "I came by because I was hoping I could get a service done."

He raises a brow. "I can tattoo you at home."

"Not a tattoo." I shake my head. "Piercing." August is licensed in body piercing, too. He's done my septum and a few on my ears. I know he also did his own nose and ears.

He tilts his head, pushing off the wall. "What do you want pierced?"

I swallow thickly, my stomach knotting in a mix of anticipation, excitement, and a little fear, too. Fear of rejection, mostly. Reaching deep, I find the confidence that only comes alive when I'm in his presence and reach for the zipper at the center of my chest. Slowly, I drag it down, opening my sweatshirt to reveal nothing but bare skin.

Something between a gasp and a moan leaves August's mouth as his jaw drops open. His pupils blow wide, chest heaving as he takes in the view of my breasts for the first time.

"Will... Will you pierce my nipples?"

Gaze completely stuck on my chest, he licks his lips several times before he speaks again. His eyes drag up to my face so slowly, it almost seems painful. "I..." He blinks at me, clearing his throat as he shakes his head. "Are... Are you sure?"

I nod.

August drags his bottom lip over his teeth, glancing at my tits again. His eyes fall closed, and he takes a deep breath, as if gathering his composure. It does fucking wonders for my ego. He shakes his head again, gesturing to the chair in the corner of the room. "Go sit down. I'll uh...I'll get the supplies."

He makes no notion to move, still staring with a bright fire blazing in his green eyes. I can't stop the smile that springs to my cheeks as I close my sweatshirt over my chest, and his gaze snaps up to mine, a faint blush running up his neck.

I walk past him, finding the chair he referenced and lying back on it. The rain outside creates a cascade of water on the windows, and the low lighting and back corner give us plenty of privacy from anyone walking by, but a small thrill races down my spine at the exposure.

August wheels over a metal tray with gloves, gauze, some kind of sanitizing solution, two needles, and two pieces of jewelry: small bars with beads on either end. His hands are shaking as he slips the black gloves on. I let my zip-up fall off my shoulders once more, baring my chest to him.

He sprays the sanitizer on a cotton pad before turning to me, voice tortured as he rasps, "You're positive about this?"

I nod but reach out to grab his forearm. "I don't want the first time you touch me like this to be with a cotton pad and gloves between your skin and mine."

August swallows. "I'm trying to be professional."

"Professionally, aren't you supposed to make sure my nipples are stimulated?"

He licks his lips. "I have a clamp."

"I don't want a clamp, Augustus. I want your hands."

"Fuck." With that, he rips the gloves off, eyes glossing as he leans over me, cupping one hand behind my neck and pulling my head toward him. He forces my gaze to his, doesn't let me look away, but I jump at the soft flick of sensation across my breast. "Is this what you wanted?"

"Yes," I breathe, that electric feeling cascading down past my stomach and settling in my core.

"Do you actually want to be pierced, Elena? Or were you looking for an excuse to get me to touch your pretty tits?" His breath skates across my jaw, sending chills down my spine as his palm flattens against my breast, squeezing deliciously.

"Both," I moan.

He laughs roughly, letting go of me as he steps back, slipping a new pair of gloves on his hands before sanitizing my skin. Knots form in my stomach as he reaches for the needle, pulling it from the sterile pouch before doing the same with the jewelry. My throat is a little dry, and my entire body is tensing in anticipation of the pain.

August unscrews one of the balls on the bar before turning back to me. "Look at me, Elena." My eyes shoot to his, and he steps over me, taking my nipple between his thumb and forefinger, rolling it back and forth. "It's just like when I did your nose and your cartilage. No different."

"I have sensitive nipples," I breathe.

He smirks. "I'll remember that for later then."

He pinches me lightly, and I gasp at the pain, though the way his eyes blaze through me, mixed with his familiar rain-and-pine scent and the feel of him touching me, sends an entirely different sensation across my skin.

Pain mixed with something primal, something I think I might crave.

Maybe it's just him.

"Keep your eyes on me, baby." *Fuck.* I like the way that sounds rolling off his lips. August nods toward me. "Play with your other tit. Look at me and touch yourself like that." There is so much heat in his gaze, I melt beneath it, brushing my thumb across my breast, my chest expanding with each rapid breath. "Does that feel good?"

I nod.

"Good." I see his hands moving, but I refuse to look at them, all my focus remains on his burning eyes and his full, wet lips—desperate to feel them on me again. "Focus on that. Focus on my voice and how good it feels to play with yourself."

His eyes drop, but before I'm able to register it, a sharp, stinging pain radiates across my flesh, followed by an excruciating burn that has me gasping.

"Sorry, baby. I'm sorry. I've got you." His voice transforms that pain into electric zaps of pleasure that gather low in my stomach, and suddenly, my clit is fucking throbbing.

August turns behind him, grabbing something off the tray before twisting the bar now through my nipple and taking a step back. The pain dulls into a low burn as my adrenaline bottoms out. "I'm going to move fast with this next one because you're anticipating it now."

I'm not sure what noise I intended to make, but it floats from my throat like a moan.

August pauses, smirking at me. "Almost sounds like you liked the pain."

"I think I liked you being the one to cause it," I say breathlessly.

"Fuck me," he whispers, grabbing his supplies as he walks around the chair. He changes his gloves, sanitizes my other breast, and pulls a fresh needle from a new pouch, along with a bar identical to the previous one.

"You're doing a good job at remaining professional, Augustus," I whimper as the cotton pad slides along my skin and the cool air pricks against my breast.

"Trust me, my thoughts are not professional."

"I'd like to hear those thoughts."

"I'll be happy to tell you about them as soon as I..." That familiar pain is blazing through my chest, my flesh on fire, tremors of it wracking my body and coiling in the center of my legs. "Finish this." He twists the jewelry against my nipple again before taking a step back and discarding his gloves.

"*Fuck.* It hurt worse that time."

August doesn't respond, placing his tools down on the metal tray and sliding it away from us. When he turns to me, his face is hard, his eyes flaming. Grabbing my hand, he interlaces our fingers, bringing them to his abdomen. He slides our hands down his stomach and presses them against the impressive bulge in his jeans.

My throat goes a little dry, the burn in my breasts temporarily forgotten as I let myself feel his hardness, his size.

"This is my *very* unprofessional reaction to your body, Elena."

I lift my head, meeting his gaze as his eyes pierce right through me, laced with lust. August has never been this bold with me before, and I find every word spilling from his mouth right now to be enticing and addictive.

"I like you unprofessional," I whisper. "I like you rough and feral." Squeezing his cock, I add, "I like you hard."

He steps around the chair, positioning himself at the center of it as he leans over me, placing his hands on the seat between my legs. He draws circles on my lower thighs with his pinkies, and the intimate touch has every atom in my body on alert.

"Are you in pain?" he asks, eyes darting to my chest behind his black glasses.

"A little." Horny more than anything else, honestly. Not sure what that says about me.

He drops his head to my jaw, pressing his lips against it. I want to grab him and force him to my lips, but I'm afraid moving my arms might hurt, and it's clear he's on some sort of mission, one I'm desperate to watch unfold.

He drags his mouth down my throat and across my chest, careful not to touch my breasts, instead kissing and suckling the skin between them, moving over my stomach as he drops to his knees on the floor in front of me.

"I can help with that," he whispers, fingers lightly skating over my jeans, like he's waiting for permission.

"August," I whisper, hardly able to catch my breath at the sight of him between my legs. "I... I normally can't..." I can't orgasm from oral. I never have. I've got specific needs that can't always be met with a mouth alone, and if I'm taking too long to come, I feel like a nuisance.

Kneeling before me, August slips off his glasses and sets them on the tray beside him, revealing enough heat in his eyes to scorch my soul. "I may not get to have all your firsts, Elena, but this is one I'll gladly claim—if you'll let me."

Fuck.

He's so dark and possessive like this, a dichotomy to the soft and timid boy I've always known, almost as if it has been awakened in him, too. He's unleashed, and all that pent up longing is zeroed in on me.

"I just... If I don't come, don't be upset."

The corner of his mouth tilts. "Baby, I'll make you come. If I have to take up permanent residence in your pussy to feel it flood my face, I'll happily move in right between these legs." He presses his lips to the denim over my thigh. "I've spent a lifetime wanting to watch you fall apart beneath me. I don't mind if you make me earn it."

My breath hitches, and all I can do is nod. Rapidly. Desperately. I'm throbbing to know what he'll feel like between my legs. His soft skin and its hint of stubble scraping along my thighs, his tongue against my clit, his fingers—*goddamn.* I need him now.

I reach for the button on my jeans, the burn across my chest a sudden reminder I am freshly pierced. August's brows raise as I pop my pants and begin to unzip them, our fingers brushing as he takes over, lowering the zipper before dipping into my waistband and pushing them down my thighs.

"Lift those hips for me, Elena." His voice is strained, like it's pure torment to go another moment without his head between my legs. He moves as quickly as I do, desperate to remove the remainder of my clothing.

Peeling my jeans off, he tosses them to the floor behind him, turning back to soak me in. I'm entirely bare to him, still lying back in the chair as he sits on the floor below me. August takes his time tracing every inch of my exposed skin, almost as if he's memorizing me.

"I'm going to draw this later," he rasps, as if I voiced those thoughts aloud. "I'm going to immortalize you like this. Fucking perfection."

Something like a whimper escapes my throat, and my knees snap together, rubbing to create friction, pressure—anything to provide relief for the need his gaze ignites in my core.

His hands shoot out, grasping my legs and spreading them

back open. His chest heaves, and his eyes go near black with lust as he lowers his gaze. August slides one hand down my thigh, eliciting sparks in his wake, before he places a featherlight touch over my pussy. He slides a finger through my slit, and my body jolts, toes curling and heart racing. He licks his lips as he uses a second finger to split me open, lightly rubbing his thumb over my clit.

"August," I sigh, back arching into his touch, desperate for more of it.

"Don't rush me, Elena," he commands. "I'm acquainting myself with this pretty little cunt of ours." He smacks my center—light and swift, just enough to set my flesh aflame. "Mhmm. I'm going to take my time with this pussy, make sure we get to know each other real well."

"Jesus Christ," I mutter, head falling back.

My eyes screw shut, fingers reaching for his soft curls, twisting in his hair. His lips move along my thigh, and I can't stop myself from bucking upward, forcing his mouth toward me. He laughs against my skin before he finally gives me what I've been craving.

I cry out as his tongue swipes through my legs, settling over my clit. He flicks over me rapidly, and a roaring sensation flies from the tips of my toes to the sparks behind my eyelids as I call out his name.

He wraps his lips around my bud, moaning as he sucks it into his mouth, almost like he's savoring me. I grip his hair, pressing his face harder against my core as I shamelessly force myself into his mouth, desperate for more pressure.

"That's it, baby," he groans. "Fuck my face. I want the pain you give, too."

I whimper at his words, the rise of ecstasy floating through my body. Chasing that peak I'm so rarely capable of achieving from clitoral stimulation alone, I gasp at the trembling in my limbs, so close to that edge I'm craving.

"Do you have any fucking clue how sweet your pussy is, Elena?" August slips his tongue into me, and it sends my back bowing off the chair, a moan tearing from my throat. "Fuck," he pulls away, "I'm so hard for you. I'm fucking pulsating just from your taste alone. You are heavenly."

I watch his hand disappear from my thigh and between his own legs. He moans, and the realization of the way I'm making him feel has my eyes rolling back, my toes curling, and my body buzzing. It's not a chore to him, not something he's doing for my benefit alone. He's genuinely enjoying this.

"Keep those legs open, baby. You close them, I stop." He removes the other hand holding my thigh in place, dragging it toward my center and teasing my opening with a finger. He slowly slips it in, pumping a few times before adding another. "Is this what you've been missing? Your needy cunt needs to be filled, doesn't it?"

Fuck. The mouth on this man is unreal.

"Yes," I whisper, struggling to keep my legs open as my body quivers around him.

He pushes deep inside me, curling his fingers and massaging the place I need him most. The sounds falling from my mouth are inhuman, the way I thrust against his face obscene, and it's when he wraps his mouth back around my clit that the elusive wave I've been chasing finally crashes against my skin, calming the fire in my veins. Sparks light behind my eyes like exploding stars, and all my senses disappear as I black out in bliss.

There is only him, only the way he makes me feel.

I'm still rocking my hips against his face as the blindness fades and I return to earth. He's moaning, muttering something like "fuck" and "goddamn", but I'm so lost in passion, I can hardly make out the sound. Finally finding the strength to lift my head, I look down to find two blazing emeralds staring back at me, flaring as if the sight of me above him is something to commit to memory.

August moves from between my thighs, sitting back on his heels. He licks his lips, as if he can't get enough of the taste of me. There's surprise in his eyes and a hint of a blush on his cheeks.

"That was..." Words are lost on me, but it's my breath that's stolen as August slowly stands and I take notice of the wet spot spread across the center of his jeans.

He bites his lip, running a hand through his hair before grabbing his glasses.

"Did you come?" I ask, lifting my gaze to meet his.

He swallows, face flushing brighter, and it might be the most erotic thing I've ever seen. "Can I be honest?"

I can't believe he has the gall to ask, considering I'm splayed out naked beneath him, my release still dripping off his lips, and he just came in his pants. "I think we're past asking that, Augustus."

A hint of a smile accents his mouth as he shakes his head. "This," he motions toward me, "is the epitome of every fantasy I've ever had. Seeing your body—inking it, piercing it, claiming you in any way I could...those were all fantasies too. But fuck, Elena, never in my wildest dreams could I allow myself to imagine what you'd look like when you come, writhing on my face, moaning my name. It was too painful—too far-fetched. I've fucked my hand to thoughts of you so many times. Seeing you in the flesh like this?" He lets out a breath. "You didn't even have to touch me."

My heart thrashes against my ribcage as my mind fights

for a response, but I'm not sure words exist for the way this feels. All my mouth is capable of producing is, "Come kiss me."

He leans over the chair, positioning himself between my legs, careful of my fresh piercings and sore chest. As he presses his lips to mine, it's wet and erotic and romantic and soft all at once.

"I can taste myself on you," I whisper into his mouth. "I like it."

He groans, "Yeah?"

"Yeah." I bite down on his lower lip, sucking my climax away. "It tastes like you belong to me."

"I've always belonged to you, Elena."

I pull back, moving slowly as I take his face between my hands, forcing his gaze to mine. His eyes pull me in like gravity, and I fall headfirst into a kaleidoscope of green.

"I belong to you, too. I think I always have."

He drops his forehead to mine, bringing one hand up to cup my face—a gesture so tender in comparison to everything else we've just done. A sigh leaves his lips, and the sound isn't sated and content like I'd expect in this moment. It's tormented, tortured, hesitant.

"Don't tell me this is a one-time thing." I laugh, but it falls flat.

August shakes his head against mine. "No, Elena. This is a forever thing." His thumbs brush against my cheeks softly. "I don't want to fuck this up. I've waited an eternity to have you like this, and I don't want to let it go."

"So don't," I whisper, grabbing his wrists.

"I don't plan on it, but I've got to talk to my brother before we go any farther. I won't have any part of you and me riddled with guilt over him."

I don't feel guilty at all. I closed the door on Zach and me the moment he closed the door to my apartment for the final time. And I padlocked it when I found out he has known for years how his brother felt about me—and manipulated us both to prevent me from choosing August.

Because if I had known, if I'd been given that choice to make, I would've chosen August. Every single fucking time. Because even when my brain was left in the dark, my soul knew something deeper existed there. He was where I felt safe, seen, and understood. He was my other half—he still is—and no part of me will ever feel guilty for finally making the right choice where my heart is concerned.

But I nod anyway, because I know at the end of the day, they're brothers, and while I know with certainty August will fight for us, I want his relationship with Zach to endure as little damage as possible.

"I understand." I smile at him, caught in the maze of his gemstone eyes.

"I know you down to the depths of your soul, but I want more than that now. I want to know how you need to be loved. I want to learn how to keep you the right way, Elena." His eyes light when he smiles back at me. "I won't touch you until I can talk to my brother. I'm going to tell him you're the love of my life, and now that you've given me a chance, I won't let go of it. I'm holding on with all I've fucking got, and until I can ensure he understands, I can't touch you again."

"You're already torturing me." I laugh breathlessly. I do understand where he's coming from, but as emotion builds behind my eyes, I realize he's what I've been waiting for all this time. He's the only person I'll ever trust to love me the right way. "I want to learn how to love you, too."

He presses his lips to my nose, and this time when he sighs against my skin, it's full of relief and conviction—full of love.

"When I love you for the first time, Elena, I'm going to do it right. I'm going to make sure it's the last first time for both of us."

Stealing a kiss from lips that seemed to have awakened the stars inside my soul, I whisper, "You'll be worth the wait."

"You've always been worth the wait," he whispers back.

Chapter Sixteen

August

Age Twenty-Three - May

"When The Night is Over" - Lord Huron

Elena's laugh is musical as I follow her out of the elevator into the top-floor suite. She scans the key against the door, pushing it open to reveal one of the most opulent hotel rooms I've ever seen. Floor-to-ceiling windows line the entirety of the space, downtown San Francisco's lights sparkling beyond them.

Plush cream couches, a modern kitchen, and a massive oak dining table accent the remainder of the living space. I follow Elena down the hallway that leads to the bedroom of the suite. I set both our bags down on a massive king-sized bed in the center of the room, accented with more windows along the left. To the right is a bathroom damn near the size of my entire apartment.

"Well, shit." Elena makes a slow circle around the room. "I guess I'm not surprised. Leo's always been a high maintenance bitch."

"He's proud of you." I laugh, coming up behind her to wrap my arms around her shoulders. She sighs contentedly, head falling onto my chest as we look out at the city beyond the windows. "We're all proud of you."

Elena took part in her first major signing as a published author this weekend. The convention had over a thousand attendees, she sat on multiple panels, and she had a line at her table the entire day. Leo booked the hotel as a gift to congratulate her for all the growth she achieved this past year.

It was the most incredible thing to see people come from all around to meet her because of how deeply they connected with the art she created. Witnessing that kind of appreciation as an artist myself, and as the person who has gotten to see her talent since the beginning, was humbling to me. It reminded me just how lucky I am to merely exist within her gravity, and it fueled my desire to make sure she never forgets how astonishing she is.

Elena glances up at me, the skyline sparkling in her dark eyes, the city lights cascading across her flawless face, but the smile she gives me is brighter than all of it.

"Didn't tell Leo I was coming, I take it?" I ask, nodding toward the one bed.

"I don't really want them asking questions yet; I don't like lying when I answer." She shrugs. "Plus, we sleep together all the time, even if we're not *sleeping* together."

We haven't told anyone about us yet, agreeing that the conversation needs to be had with Zach first. I tried spitting it out the first few times I spoke with him on the phone after Elena and I started...whatever this is, but I couldn't do it. He deserves more than a phone conversation during our brief, once-a-week check-ins. At the end of this summer, Zach will come back home. Whether to stay or to visit, we aren't sure yet. He's not sure either. He doesn't know what he wants to do after his stint in Wyoming, and he's in no rush to decide, but he promised he'll come visit for at least a little while.

Not touching Elena until then is more than enough punishment for any betrayal my brother will feel—especially when she looks at me the way she does right now. She is unearthly beautiful, melting into my arms like she was always meant to be there, letting down her prickly exterior to reveal the soft woman inside only I have ever known.

Not to mention, I still can't get her fucking taste out of my mouth. I think about her writhing against my tongue every time I close my eyes. I see it every time I get myself off—outside the times when she's doing the same on a video call, or when she sends me naked photos of herself.

That's how we've gotten by these last few months: a few stolen kisses, a bit of dry humping, and a whole lot of fucking phone sex. As painful as it is sometimes, I relish it too. It feels like we're teenagers, like we're forbidden. It feels like how our youth should've gone all along. I was supposed to be that person for her, and if I couldn't be that back then, I get to be it now.

"Augustus," she whispers, breaking me from my thoughts.

"Hmm?"

"I said," she laughs lightly, stepping out from my arms and crossing the room, "I'm going to take a bath."

Fuck. I'm instantly hard.

She turns back to me, lust laced in her gaze. "You wanna join?"

"Baby, I thought I told you to stop propositioning me. I don't have the self-control for that."

She only raises a brow as she reaches behind her neck and grasps the zipper of the tight black dress she's wearing. "I thought I told you to stop calling me baby."

"Just slips out." My lips tilt upward.

"Oh, do you mean the same way this dress..." She unzips it all the way, allowing it to fall off her shoulders and pool around her legs on the floor, leaving her standing in front of me in nothing but silk panties and a black bra. "Just slipped off?"

I swallow thickly. My cock throbs and my heart pounds against my chest, seizing the air from my lungs. "Why do you have to tease me like this?"

She smiles, reaching behind her back and unclasping her bra. It falls to the floor with her dress. Her piercings glint in the light outside the window, and my body is on fucking fire.

"I'm an agent of chaos." She smirks at me innocently, shrugging as her hair falls over her shoulder, and it's the most stunning thing I've ever seen.

She's the definition of chaos, and I'm fucking addicted to it.

She's always teasing me like this, and I know she respects what I'm trying to do regarding my brother. I also know she doesn't feel an ounce of guilt herself; if I gave the green light right now, she'd fuck me until the sun came up. I've never been wanted like that before. Craved and desired. It makes it that much harder to hang on.

Because in Elena's mind, it's already her and me. We're permanent, our names etched into the fabric of the universe side-by-side. Everything could blow up when Zach returns home and our families find out about us, but she doesn't care. That's her chaos, her recklessness. We've chosen each other, and everything else is secondary.

It's why I love her. But part of the reason I've held back is because I can't help the glimpse of fear that as soon as Zach returns home, as soon as she's in his presence again, she'll go back to him. Just like she always did. It's self-preservation, keeping some piece of my soul intact. Because once I have her fully, once our bodies join that way, everything that already feels permanent will be cemented. She'll absorb my soul, and there will be no recovery. I can't give her that if any chance remains she'll choose him in the end.

"Welp, I'm going to go get in the tub. All hot water and bare skin. Too bad you're going to miss—" I reach out, snatching

Elena behind her neck and tugging her into me, hearing the surprised breath leave her lungs at the rapid movement.

Her bare chest crushed against mine, she looks up at me with those hooded, impassioned eyes that drive me mad. She's too fucking enticing like this. Too tempting. A siren luring me in. I twist my fingers in her hair, and she hisses at the hint of pain, just enough to make her drip for me. "One of these days, Elena, I'm going to make you pay for all this teasing." I drop my head, breathing against her ear as I take it between my teeth. "I'm going to edge you until your pussy isn't the only thing crying for me. I'm going to spend days on you, breaking you, until you forget everything except what it feels like to beg for me."

I feel the chills that race up her spine, the goose bumps that rise on the nape of her neck, the small gasp that leaves her lips.

I pull away, searching her eyes for a sign I've gone too far, but all I find is desire and darkness staring back at me. "You've gotten to tattoo me, pierce me. You've claimed me," she whispers. Wedging her hand between our bodies, she drags it down my stomach. "I want to claim you, too."

I snatch her wrist just before it reaches my waistband. "You've claimed me, Elena." In more ways than she could ever understand.

She shakes out of my hold, pressing her palm against my cock. *Always fighting me.* And fuck, I revel in it. "I want to taste you," she rasps. She reaches behind her head with her free hand, unlocking my grip in her hair, and I let it happen. I let her fall to her knees in front of me, brushing both hands over my dick now, looking up at me with those endless brown eyes, desperation in her gaze.

I could come from the sight of that alone.

"It won't take days, Augustus. I'm ready to beg for it right now." She bites her lip, batting her lashes. I'm fucking weak in the knees when she says, "Can I taste you? Please?"

"Fuck," I groan, closing my eyes and tilting my head back. *This fucking woman.* "I can't fuck you yet, Elena. I can't go that far."

"I didn't ask for that." Her voice is soft, timid, such a contrast to the spitfire I'm used to. I adore this secret side of her—submissive, but just for me. "I want you to fuck my mouth, take a bath with me, and rub my back while I fall asleep. That's it. Don't deny me that, baby. Please."

Christ.

I nod once, and she's on me. Her fingers brush against my cock, leaving it pulsing as she slowly undoes my belt, slipping it through the loops and tossing it aside. She makes quick work of my jeans, tugging them down my legs, and I know the exact moment she sees what I've been hiding for years as her movement stills and her breath catches.

I glance down at her, watching as she holds one hand to her mouth, eyes blazing with shock, while her other hand slowly skates across the ink displayed upon my upper thigh.

Her name, written three times in a column, each with a different font.

"Augustus," she gasps, lifting her gaze to mine.

I swallow, unsure of her reaction. "I did them myself years ago. I was practicing."

Her hand falls to her chest, as if she's clutching her raging heart. "Why my name?"

"Yours is the only name I knew I'd want to die with on my flesh." I reach down, gripping her chin and forcing her to raise her gaze again. "I told you, Elena—you claimed me long ago."

She licks her lips, eyes smoldering with need. I can't help

myself from extending my thumb so it catches on her tongue, forcing her to taste my skin.

"How often have you imagined me on my knees for you?"

A shaky breath leaves my lips. "More than I care to admit."

Her hands trail up my thighs, achingly slow, before dipping into my waistband. "I want to be your fantasy," she rasps quietly. Pulling my underwear down my legs, her breath hitches again. The sound is different this time—not just shock, but desperation. Need.

Her jaw drops, chest heaving as her eyes take in my cock—hard and raging. She drags her eyes to my face. "Take your shirt off," she demands, and I immediately comply. She absorbs me towering above her in nothing at all. Licking her lips, she smiles. "You're a fucking masterpiece."

My cock jumps, eyes rolling back at her praise. Her laugh is salacious as she brushes a hand over me, wrapping around my base and pumping hard enough to send me gasping.

"I want you to show me what you imagine when you close your eyes, Augustus. We're not at home. This isn't Pacific Shores. In this room, we can live inside our dreams." She grabs my hand, forcing it to the back of her head. "Use my mouth the way you've only been able to inside your mind. Keep them open this time; watch me while I bring your fantasies to life."

"Elena," I groan, watching as she brings her mouth to my cock. Her eyes never leave mine as her tongue darts out from between her lips, tasting me for the first time. Pleasure zips down my spine, spreading through my veins as she wraps her lips around me entirely.

She moans, the sound vibrating against my cock as she takes me deeper. I reach resistance at the back of her throat, but she continues pushing. Heat licks up my flesh as she sputters, wrapping her tongue around my base and bobbing her head.

I twist my fingers in her thick curls, holding her in place as I begin to pump in and out of her mouth.

I thrust until her throat tightens, then go a step farther until she's choking. She doesn't close her eyes, keeping them glued to mine. I watch them water over, mascara running down her cheeks as I ruin her.

My body tightens at the sight of it, and I fuck her face harder, faster. She takes all of it, gagging and sputtering around my cock as spit drips down the sides of her lips, ropes of it keeping us connected each time I pull out of her mouth. I see the desire building in her eyes—she likes being used like this.

"You love choking on it, don't you, Elena?"

She moans, nodding through her tears.

"I wish you could see yourself like this. I've made a fucking mess of you. You look so pretty, drooling on my cock. My perfect little whore." Her eyes grow heavy at my words, and I can see her fingers inch down her thighs, like she's fighting not to touch herself. I smile. "Are you waiting for my permission to play with your greedy cunt, baby?"

I pause at the back of her throat, my cock pulsing in her mouth as she attempts to nod.

"You think you deserve the right to come?" I ask, voice thick and strained with pleasure. "I thought I said something earlier about punishing you for being such a fucking tease." She moans again, the sound stemming from frustration more than pleasure. "But you're such a good girl, being so obedient for me. I bet if I told you not to, you'd go all night without touching your pussy, wouldn't you? You'd let me edge you until you were dripping over the floor. Isn't that right?"

I start fucking her mouth again, knowing she's attempting to nod, but I tighten my grip on her hair, holding her head still. I thrust deep before pulling out completely. She sucks in a rapid breath of air, gasping, "Please—", but I force my cock inside her mouth again before she has the chance to finish. I repeat the former movement, giving her a chance to say, "Let—" I thrust again, "Me—" she speaks through each push into her mouth, "Come."

I exit her mouth one final time, and the words spill from it so quickly, I don't have the chance to shut her up again before she says, "Daddy, please. Let me touch my greedy cunt. Let me come with you."

Fucking hell. I pull her hair, bringing her mouth over me again, and she takes it hungrily. "I swear to God, woman, you're going to be the death of me." I feel her laugh, as if she knows she just got exactly what she wanted out of me. "Play with your pussy, baby. Make yourself feel good while I use your slutty fucking mouth."

She whimpers, her hand disappearing between her thighs. Her eyes flutter, fighting to remain open as she begins to strum her clit. We don't break contact, though, both chasing that ecstasy through one another.

It's otherworldly with her. I never imagined it could be like this with anyone, but I've always known the highest peaks of pleasure could only be found in her arms. I haven't even been inside her yet, and she has exceeded every fucking expectation.

That primal, red-hot need gathers at the base of my spine. My cock pulses in her mouth—I'm getting close. I see her hand moving faster, and I know she's nearing that edge too.

"Come for me, Elena. Now. Please," I whimper, my legs growing weak as the pleasure builds. Her mouth opens wider as a moan floats out of it, her thighs trembling beneath her. Watching her come undone is all it takes for me to unleash with her. I pull out, gripping the head of my cock. "Stick out your tongue," I command.

She obeys, and I position myself at her mouth as I explode. Light bursts in my periphery, and the world goes hazy as I spill myself across her lips and onto her tongue.

"Do not swallow," I growl, dropping my dick to grip her chin as I float back down from my orgasm. "Hold it. Show me."

Her eyes flare as she sticks her tongue out farther, my release pooling in her mouth and dripping down her chin. A fierce satisfaction rushes through me at the sight of her.

"Your mouth looks so pretty full of my cum." I squat down, swiping two fingers across her tongue, then dragging them over her chin and throat. I continue the descent down her chest, circling each one of her nipples, leaving a glistening trail of moisture in my wake. My touch is featherlight as I whisper across her clit, sending her gasping. "Bet your tight little cunt would look even better filled up."

Quickly, I slide those two fingers inside her, and she moans at the intrusion. I pump a few times, quivers wracking her body. Pulling out, I suck my fingers clean, savoring the heady taste of our mixed releases on my skin. "Tastes like you're mine."

Makeup streaks down her cheeks, her eyes blazing as she watches me. Her tongue still out, my release drips down her chin and onto the floor between her knees. The trail of it glitters on her skin in the bright lights of the city beyond the windows.

"Looks like you're mine too." I grasp her jaw, forcing her mouth closed. "Swallow my cum, Elena, and remember that. There's no going back from this now that I've let you ruin me."

I watch her throat work, licking the final remnants of me from her lips.

"You ruined me, too," she breathes.

Chapter Seventeen

Elena

Age Twenty-Five - September

"The Black Dog" - Taylor Swift

"Hey, Rosebud."

The voice, smooth as butter, grates on my ears like I'm a block of cheese. An all-too-familiar hand slides a copy of my latest release across the table in front of me, like he's just another reader in line for a signature.

I lift my head, clashing against depthless brown eyes I used to think I'd never find my way out of. He's rougher than he was the last time I saw him—calluses on his hands that weren't there before, a deep, golden tan from being outdoors for days on end. He's got a few days' worth of patchy scruff shadowing his jaw—he's never been good at growing a beard.

"You're home," I say flatly.

"I just landed in San Diego. Everett said you were doing a signing down here, so I thought I'd stop by before I head back to my parents' house."

Someone in line behind him clears their throat, and I quickly grab the book, scribbling down the first personalization that comes to mind:

For: Asshole

xoxo,

I add my Violet Rose signature and slide it back, knowing he'll probably toss it in the trash on his way out. "As in-character as it is for you to show up at one of my signings and expect my undivided attention, I'm here for my readers. I don't have time to do this right now."

Zach's expression turns crestfallen. "I just wanted to stop by and see you in action. I think it's cool to see how loved you are, Ele—Violet." He takes the signed book, clutching it to his chest. "Do you think you could find some time for us to talk?"

I glance around the bookstore, eyeing the parking lot beyond its doors. "This signing is done in an hour." I nod toward the sports bar across the street. "If you wait for me there, I'll stop by before I head home."

He smiles hopefully. "Should I have a Dirty Shirley ready for you?"

"I hold zero embarrassment for my alcoholic beverages of choice, Zachary," I mutter, turning to the reader behind him in line. He laughs as he strolls away, and because some old habits are impossible to kill, I can't stop the way my lips tilt up at the sound.

An hour and a half later—because I'm a liar and wanted to see if he'd actually wait—I stroll into a building labeled *Sharkies* expecting it to be void of childhood loves.

Instead, I'm greeted by the sight of Zach sitting at the bar, worn boots propped up on the stool, and my dark, taboo mafia romance book in his hand. He's so focused on the pages, he doesn't notice when I sit down next to him.

"Have you fallen in love with Dimitri yet?" I ask, referencing my main male character.

Zach's head snaps up, a surprised smile on his face. "I thought you bailed, but I was enjoying it so much, I figured I'd hang out for a while just in case." He shuts the book and slides my drink toward me. Most of the ice has melted by now, condensation dripping from the glass like the trepidation cascading down the tightly locked walls around my heart. "Dimitri is very dreamy." Zach laughs. "Are you getting any real-life inspiration for the men in your books these days?"

Oh, okay, so we're just going to jump into this conversation.

"No." I scoff, taking a sip. "Believe it or not, it's actually my imagination alone that inspires the characters I create."

"Sorry." He clears his throat. "That was a lame segue to ask if you're with someone."

"How about asking me how I'm doing, Zach? How about you ask me how many months I cried myself to sleep over you?" I slam my glass on the counter, turning to face him head-on. "Or, at the very least, why don't you tell me if Wyoming was worth all of that? Was it everything you hoped it'd be?"

Zach refuses to meet my eyes, peeling the label off his beer bottle as he says, "Saying that would make me feel a lot less guilty if I knew you were happy now, too."

I laugh, and all the pain I expect to rage against my chest doesn't come. In fact, all I feel is relief. "I'm very happy." I grab his arm, forcing him to lift his head and see my smile. "I really am."

He exhales, placing his hand over mine and squeezing.

"Now, tell me how Wyoming really was."

The biggest grin I've ever seen on him spreads across his cheeks. "It was...incredible. The work was hard, and I was never not tired. The first few weeks were absolutely miserable, but once I realized waking up before dawn meant you never missed the sunrise, I actually started to get excited about it. Sitting out there, watching the sun come up over the mountains like that..." He continues, detailing every aspect of his life working on a cattle ranch.

I'll be honest, not one bit of it sounds like a good time to me—except maybe the sunrise over the mountains, but I get ocean sunsets every single day. I'm not sure mucking horseshit or whatever the fuck else he had to do is worth that when all I have to do is look out my window.

"So, are you going back?" I ask once he finishes. The bartender moves to make me another drink, but I stop her. I need to head back to Pacific Shores and track down August before Zach does. I don't think he told anyone he was coming home.

"I don't think so. I loved it out there. It gave me everything I needed, helped me figure out who I want to be." He shrugs. "But it wasn't home. Pacific Shores is home."

I nod, and those knots I thought I'd avoided earlier finally twist in my gut. If Zach is here to stay, I don't know what that means for August and me. Sitting in front of him now, I feel nothing like I used to, outside of appreciation for his physical form.

I think I'll always consider Zach my first love—he earned that title. The all-consuming, burning, lose-your-mind kind of obsession between two young people exploring the concept of intimacy for the first time isn't something to overlook or belittle. Still, when I look back now, I realize, I'm not sure I was ever *in* love with him. No, I was infatuated.

I wasn't able to tell the difference between the two until I experienced the real thing, and now that I've fallen for August, nothing else would ever measure up.

Regardless, the dynamic between the three of us will have consequences, and I don't know what Zach staying in Pacific Shores is going to stir up.

"I'm heading out to my parents' place in Palm Springs for a couple of weeks to spend some time with them, recover and relax from the past year." He drains the remainder of his beer. "Then, I'm going to move home and head back to school."

"School?" I ask. "For what?"

"I want to be a teacher. A coach, too. I worked with some kids, giving horseback riding lessons my last few months out there, and I realized I'm really damn good with them. Plus, playing sports always gave me a purpose, and I want to find that again." He smiles proudly. "I'm finally ready to get my life together. Gonna work with the guys at the surf shop and offer lessons while I finish my degree."

I slide off the barstool, throwing my purse over my shoulder as I grasp Zach's arm. "I'm proud of you. I'm glad you found what you were looking for out there." I squeeze it gently before pulling back to head toward the door.

He catches my wrist quickly, forcing me to turn around. "My door's still open for you, Elena." Zach brushes his thumb across my skin. "I don't expect anything, but I just want you to know that."

I softly pull out of his grasp, offering a sorry smile. "I'm in someone else's room now."

I don't wait to see his reaction before I turn around, heading out of the dark bar into the bright daylight.

August

"All right, just hear me out." Zach walks a few steps ahead of me, between the alley of two residential roads in town that we have no ties to. "I've been saving up damn near every penny I've made the last year, mostly for college, but..." My brother stops in front of a two-story, Craftsman style house, turning to face me with a smile. "I bought us a house."

"What?" I blink, all other words lost on me.

Zach has been staying with our parents in Palm Springs the last couple of weeks. I drove out there this weekend to spend time with them, and Zach and I came back to Pacific Shores together. I haven't told him about Elena and me yet, although I know Elena told him she moved on and was with someone else now.

He asked me about it once. I told him it wasn't my place to speak for her, and he hasn't brought it up again since.

My plan was to tell Zach today and then race over to Elena's apartment, get lost in her perfect fucking body, and beg her to move in with me. Because she's my future. She has always been my future, and my brother has always been a fucking roadblock.

"*Us?*" I ask.

Zach laughs, nodding. "Yeah. I mean, I'll cover the down payment, and Mom co-signed the home loan, but I bought it for both of us."

"Zach." I rub my forehead, despair funneling through my body. "I... I don't know."

"C'mon, I know you don't want to live in that shitty studio above the shop. This house is great!" He throws his arms out. "It's got plenty of space, a yard for kick-backs, and it even has a sunroom. I was thinking you could turn it into an art studio since I know you still love to draw. There is a den downstairs that would be the perfect little library for you. Elena could use it, too." He shrugs. "If she wants."

Fuck me.

I have been staying in the studio space above my tattoo shop. It works well enough, with space for a bed and a couch. It doesn't have a full kitchen, but all I really need is a microwave anyway. The worst part is the lack of a shower, but it has a bathroom, so I've just been bathing at my parents' house every day. I didn't look for a place upon my permanent move back to Pacific Shores because I was hoping Elena and I would find one together.

Zach steps up to me, placing his hands on my shoulders. "We haven't gotten to live together as adults, and I think we could have a lot of fun before we both settle down. Plus, you're the person I missed most while I was away. I'm ready to plant roots in my hometown. I may not have someone to plant them with yet, so in the meantime, I might as well spend as much time as possible with my favorite person."

I swallow, thorns of guilt sluicing through my veins and tearing my skin apart. Looking past my brother to the house behind him, I have no clue how I'm going to make it out of this with all our hearts intact. All I can seem to do right now is force a smile back. "Show me the inside."

Chapter Eighteen

Elena

October First

"How Did It End?" - Taylor Swift

My characters are driving me up a fucking wall right now.

No matter what words filter through my brain, into my fingers, and onto the screen in front of me, they aren't right. I can't figure out where I want to go with this story, and the figments of my imagination are being incredibly difficult to work with.

I sigh, fishing a sweet pickle out of the jar on my desk and popping it into my mouth. I always keep pickles nearby when I'm writing because, well, I love them. Plus, the crunch and the vinegar taste help me stay awake when I'm working late nights like this. It's a quarter past midnight, and I'm only about a third through my word goal for today.

I crack my neck, setting my hands back down on my keyboard—when the rasp of knuckles on my front door distracts me. I don't know who the fuck would be showing up at my apartment unannounced at this time of night. August has an early start tomorrow at the Boardwalk, which is why he isn't here right now, and I'm fairly certain he fell asleep about an hour ago.

Neither my parents nor my brothers would show up this late without calling first, and I don't have any other friends.

That only leaves two possibilities: a very polite axe-murderer, or Zachary Hayes.

Not sure which I fear more.

I pad to the front of the room, peering through the peephole to find Zach standing outside. I throw the door open, and I can immediately tell he has been drinking. His eyes are glossed over and bloodshot, his clothes crinkled, his hair a mess.

"Please tell me you didn't drive here."

He shakes his head. "Ubered from the bar."

I step aside, letting him through. "Went out with your brothers tonight." He walks into the center of my kitchen before turning to face me. "You told me you moved on. You're with someone, right?"

"Yes," I whisper, shutting the door and leaning against it.

"Why don't your brothers know anything about it then? I asked them how they felt about your new boyfriend, and they had no fucking clue who I was talking about."

"Let's go sit down." I reach toward him, intending to take his hand and lead him to the couch, but he steps back.

"What secrets are you hiding, Elena?"

I tilt my head. "Why does it matter to you?"

A faraway look casts over Zach's eyes. "I don't know." He shakes his head, beginning to pace. "I don't know, and I hate it. I fucking hate it."

"Hate what?" I ask softly.

He stops abruptly, running a hand through his hair as he looks at me, brown eyes burning holes through my soul. "I can't stop feeling like you're mine, wondering who the fuck else has been touching you, if they've been loving you in all the ways I never could."

I swallow through the swelling in my throat, tears stinging my eyes. I force my way into Zach's space. "You're drunk." I take his hand, pulling him toward the hallway. "You can sleep in the guest room, and we'll sort all this out tomorrow when your head is clear."

He sighs, defeated, dragging his feet as I bring him to Leo's old bedroom and softly push him onto the bed. He lies back, placing a hand over his eyes as I take off his shoes and throw the comforter over him.

Leo has been living in one of the studios above the surf shop, since they spend so much time there—and I no longer rely on his income to pay my rent. I've turned his old bedroom into an office, but I kept a bed for nights my brothers stay over late and need a place to crash.

"Any chance I can get you to lie down with me?" Zach whispers as I shut off the light.

"Not anymore. Goodnight, Zach," I murmur back, closing the door softly.

"Is it my brother?"

His voice startles me, coming from behind where I stand at the kitchen counter. Dread barrels through me, afraid he'll see the look on my face and read my every thought, I don't turn around.

"What do you mean?" I ask, feigning nonchalance as I pour two mugs of coffee, his with a small splash of milk and mine with a heaping dump of oat milk creamer.

"The person loving you in all the right ways—is it my brother?"

"Zach." I sigh, chest growing tight, sadness rushing through me like a rogue ocean wave.

I turn around, holding his coffee out to him like a peace offering. He doesn't take it.

"You were wearing his shirt last night. And you smelled like his cologne."

Rain and pine. The scent has soaked into all his clothes, and it's the reason I keep them.

I stare at the floor, not bothering to offer a response. There's nothing to say. I don't owe him anything, but that doesn't mean I'm rooting for his pain.

"How long?"

"Since January," I whisper.

A snide laugh leaves his mouth. "Kind of repulsive, no? His hands. Mouth. His dick. Touching and tasting all the places I've already been?"

My skin crawls at his insinuation—that I'm something to be owned, that he marked his territory, that any other touch is a desecration of an object he already claimed.

"We haven't—"

"Are you that desperate, Elena? For my attention? For *any* attention? Whoring yourself out to anyone who will give you the time of day?"

Flames rage through my veins. I lift my head, meeting his stare, unflinching. "Excuse me?"

His jaw clenches. "It could've been anyone else. *Anyone else*."

"No, Zach. I don't think it could," I snap. "Because it doesn't seem to matter when you've already decided I'm a piece of fucking property to you."

"You never would've ended up with him if I hadn't left."

I smile, because what I say next will break him—and I can never seem to stop myself from spewing the venom. "Thank God you did then, right? Maybe you should go again. For good this time?"

His face twists in pain. It's not the anger or the fury I'm

used to when we battle like this. No, it's a genuine defeat. I'm witnessing Zach give up right in front of my eyes, and while part of me wants to weep for it, it's relief that washes through me.

We're one step closer to putting all this behind us. He's one step closer to acceptance.

"You called it right," I whisper. "He loves me in all the ways you never could. For the first time, I realized what being in love actually feels like. I'm just sorry you and I got caught up in our shit for as long as we did. I should've chosen him from the start. I would've saved all of us a lot of pain. So," I shrug, "I'll apologize for that much."

He nods, disbelief and utter devastation pouring over his features. "You know, I did try. I really did." He spins on his heel, grasping the door handle before tossing one last sentence in my direction—the one that'll shatter me. "But you are impossible to love."

Without another word, Zachary Hayes walks out of my life once again. The door slams as I slide to the floor, finally allowing my tears to spill, because something about the echo of it clamoring through my chest feels final.

Chapter Nineteen

August

October Second

"epiphany" - Taylor Swift

"You fucked my girlfriend?"

My brother's voice rages against the back of my head. I quickly rise and turn to face him. The wind gusts across our faces, causing the waves to crash harder against the sand behind us.

"She's not your girlfriend."

He scoffs, eyes bulging. "That's all you have to say?"

"We haven't had sex yet."

Zach's jaw trembles, and he looks away as he scoffs. "For *months,* Augustus. *Months.* Behind my back and lying to my fucking face."

"I didn't lie to your face," I say softly. "I lied into your ears because I felt it was best to tell you in person. I wanted to wait until you got home."

"So you've been sneaking around with her? Keeping it from everyone?"

"It wouldn't have been fair to ask our family or friends to lie to you, too."

"Thanks so much for taking that into consideration." He laughs, but it's humorless. "Why her? Of every woman on this goddamn planet, why her?"

"If you're asking that question, it proves exactly why you never deserved her to begin with."

It's almost imperceptible, but his face softens.

"Admit it. You only loved her because she was mine first."

"Bullshit." I roll my eyes, unwilling to even entertain that idea. "I did not love her *because* of you. I loved her in *spite* of you. Every time you broke her heart and she came to me with tears streaming down her face, I fixed it, knowing she'd go crawling back to you. For years, I watched you ruin each other, and I stayed back—because I prioritized both of your happiness over my own.

"So, no. I will not apologize to you. I will not feel guilty for repairing what you broke, for cherishing what you threw away." I toss my board down at our feet, taking a step toward him. "I know you're angry with me right now. I know you feel betrayed, and I understand it. I understand it because you've made me feel that way too." I point at him, nearly close enough to poke his chest. "So you can rage right now. You can hit me if you need to, but eventually, I need you to understand—it was always going to be her and me, and we're *all* gonna be better for it."

"I do see it, Augustus. I've always fucking seen it," he seethes. "And that fucking sucks. Because Elena was the *one thing* that was supposed to be mine. Just mine."

"The only person Elena is supposed to belong to is herself."

Zach huffs, nodding tersely. He's quiet for a moment, like he's trying to quell his roaring anger. He paces a bit before finally walking over to my board and throwing his down beside it, along with his bag.

"You're my brother, and I'll get over this eventually, but it's going to take me a while before I can apologize to Elena for the things I said this morning. I can't say I regret them quite yet."

"This morning?" My tone suggests surprise, but more than that, it suggests betrayal. I haven't spoken to Elena yet today, but I assumed she was sleeping in after a late-night writing session.

Zach catches onto that slip, smirking as he squats to wax his board. "Oh? She didn't tell you? I slept over there last night."

Desolation ravages me, twisting my stomach and shoving it up my throat, cutting off my air.

"What? Don't you trust her?" Zach knows the question is loaded. In every situation, I trust Elena implicitly. I trust her more than anyone I've ever known. The only thing that can shake our solid foundation is the person standing in front of me, the person who slept beneath her roof last night.

"It's a bad day for surfing. We should go another time." My words are flat and broken as I pick up my board and take off through the sand, knowing I'm not going to calm the storm rumbling beneath my skin until I get her explanation and have her in my arms.

"August!" my brother calls. "That was a joke. C'mon. Where are you going?"

"I've got to make sure she's okay." I turn around, facing my brother as he stands and begins walking after me. "I have no doubt you left damage in your wake." I don't say another word, climbing the stairs that ascend the cliffside this beach rests beneath. I refuse to look back, rage rushing through my veins. For a moment, I almost wish he'd just disappear. It's a fleeting thought, but I can't stop it from whispering the desire to have him absent from our lives again. I can't ignore how much destruction he's caused Elena and me in the short time he has been back.

The thought fades. I don't know how we'll get our happy ending in my brother's presence, but I can't see any of us finding a happily ever after without it either. He's my brother, my family, part of all of us, and as fucked-up as this whole dynamic has become, I know deep down, none of us would ever truly be better off without him.

I reach the top, fastening my board to the roof of my Bronco. As if a breath skates across my neck, some sensation has me spinning, facing the horizon. The sky is dark, swirling, black clouds circling like some kind of omen. The water is choppy, waves hurling against the shore.

It's a bad day for surfing. We never should've come out today.

I scan the sand for my brother, about to shout that warning once again, except I don't see him on the shore. His bag is still there, dog walkers and beachgoers stroll the coastline.

I scan the water, heart stalling as I become desperate for any sight of him. His dark hair, his red surfboard—any proof at all that he's still where I left him. I come up empty.

The ocean is a raging abyss of blue. No end. No mercy. It's a bad day for surfing, yet I know with bone-deep conviction that my brother went out into those waves anyway, and now, he's nowhere to be found.

Chapter Twenty

Elena

October Second - Evening

"Indigo (featuring Avery Anna)" - Sam Barber

4 missed calls

Everett

Answer the phone.

2 missed calls

Leo

Where are you?

2 missed calls

Everett

Can you meet at the emergency room? ASAP. Something happened.

Chapter Twenty-One

Elena

Two Weeks After

"Love Letter From The Sea To The Shore" - Delaney Bailey

"*Mi corazón.*" My father's soft hand rubs my back, pulling me from my haze. "How are you feeling today?"

I can't feel anything at all. I can't feel how hollow my stomach is, let alone the gaping hole in my chest where my heart used to be. It's as if I've been drowning in my own blood for days on end, but it just won't kill me.

Drowning. Killing. Death.

I almost want to laugh at the metaphors I can't stop voicing in my head. I guess as a writer, my mind works in comparisons, ways to describe life as something more beautiful. The Earth, the sun, the stars, and the sea.

Until metaphors aren't metaphors anymore, and everything turns dark.

"I'm okay," I murmur. There's no point in explaining these thoughts; he wouldn't understand them anyway.

Nobody really understands my mind to begin with, and with the secrets I'm harboring now, they never will. Explaining this void I exist within would only serve to concern my parents. They'd try to fix me, and I'm past being fixed. I'm so broken, I've been ground to dust on the wind—scattered across the sky, never to be recovered.

"Do you want to go for a walk?" he asks quietly.

"No, I'm tired."

"You haven't gotten out of bed in days." Leo's voice comes from slightly farther away. "The funeral is tomorrow. You'll at least go to that, right?"

I don't respond. Words like funeral insist there is something to mourn, something to miss. I don't deserve either of those things.

Silence stretches on before my brother sighs.

I know I'm disappointing them. I know they're hurting too, but they're still getting up every day to take care of the Hayes family, to plan and prepare for what comes next. For all the destruction I've caused, I should be helping too, but it's not often monsters are invited to the cleanup in the wake of their wreckage.

"August stopped by. He's downstairs. He'd like to talk to you, if you're okay with that."

The faintest spark of feeling ignites from whatever shards of my being stayed behind after I walked into that emergency room—rage and regret, despair and guilt and betrayal.

We don't say his name, not once since we left the hospital that day.

The family. *The* funeral. *The* remains.

But never his name. It's supposed to be too painful, but all I feel is numb.

The sound of a summer month is what tears across my flesh like a flaming knife. It's *that* name finally giving me the sensation of choking on my own blood as it pools in my throat.

"No." The word tears from my lips—broken and raw, full of emotion I can't seem to feel over anything else.

And *that* is why I won't see him, won't speak of him or to him, won't allow myself to think about him or consider his name. Zach is fucking dead, and I feel nothing. That hole is like a chamber inside my chest, echoing our final words.

And. I. Feel. Nothing.

It's Zach's brother who's like gauze to the open wound inside my soul. I know he'd hear me, see me. He wouldn't let me become consumed by this guilt alone. He'd share this grief and this fear. He'd forgive me. He'd still love me, despite it all.

And I don't deserve that.

This guilt isn't his to forgive, and it's solely mine to hold.

I deserve nothing.

Chapter Twenty-Two

August

Three Months After

"would've been you" - sombre

I almost don't get up to answer the door. It's not worth the effort. It's not my parents. They've taken up permanent residence in Palm Springs—not that they'd come by even if they were still here.

It's not Leo. He's already off competing again, burying himself in work, I assume. The same way Everett has been pouring himself into two businesses, which makes him the unlikely visitor at this hour, too.

I wouldn't answer it—except I continue to hold out hope for the one person it could be, the person I should've given up on weeks ago. By all appearances, I have. I stopped showing up at Everett's apartment. I stopped calling her. I stopped asking her mother how she's doing.

When she didn't show her face at the funeral, that was my final straw.

All the pain I imagined her enduring...she had to know I was feeling it too. The same intensity, the same guilt, the same isolation. I needed her this time. We needed each other.

And she disappeared.

Maybe it's because I'm a glutton for punishment, or because I'm a hopeless romantic, but either way, I peel myself off the couch. Unending reruns of *The Office* play on my television behind me as I pad to the living room of my new house. I toss the front door open—and I'm startled by caramel-colored eyes.

Eyes once full of mischief, wonder, and affection are instead lifeless and empty. All hollowed cheeks and pale skin, she's thinner than I've ever seen her, almost like a walking corpse.

"Elena." The gasp that leaves my lips is raw with shock and fear.

Her face crumbles at the sound, heavy tears spilling from her eyes as she cups her face, shoulders heaving with sobs. It's an innate instinct to reach out and grab her, to pull her inside and crush her against my chest.

I run my hand down the back of her head, smoothing out her hair. "It's okay, baby. You're all right."

"Nothing...will...ever..." she heaves between sobs, "be... okay again."

"I know," I whisper.

She only cries harder, but I have nothing else to give her. The world I built my life inside, the only reality I've ever known, is gone. I don't know where to go from here—where any of us go from here. It doesn't feel right to live without him, to move forward beyond the guilt and pain and emptiness.

I think about his lack of existence, and I spiral. It's something that, after three months, I still don't know how to comprehend. It's the absence of someone you never prepared yourself to live without, someone who had goals and aspirations, feelings and plans and an entire fucking life to live.

No. Things will never be okay again.

And maybe I don't deserve it, but I let myself sink into the sea of her embrace. I allow the scent of her, warm and spiced, the pressure of her body, to hold me in place. She's still my gravity. Maybe I'm wrong to hope, and maybe I don't deserve to crave any other outcome than the one I'm residing in now, but when Elena's in my arms, it feels like one of the universe's many wrongs has been righted.

I bracket her hips, lifting her. She wraps her legs around my waist, clinging to me like a lifeline as I carry her up the stairs into my bedroom. I set her down on the edge of the bed, and she pulls back to look at me. Her face is so broken, but a flicker of light glitters in her gaze as she cups my face, running a thumb across my cheek.

"August..." she whispers.

I wait for her to continue, to say the words her soul begs to speak. I can see them behind the veil in her eyes.

But she never does, so I slowly peel her leggings down, leaving her in only underwear. I slide my hand up her back beneath the oversized tee she's wearing, unclasping her bra. I drag the straps down her arms and through the sleeves before she pulls it free and tosses it to the floor.

Reaching for the hem of my shirt, she lifts it, and I help her take it off before I strip down to my underwear. I move to crawl into bed, but Elena puts a hand on my chest, pausing to run her eyes over my body. She brushes the constellation on my wrist. Her sign. Her name on my thigh. Violets inked across my collarbone, my entire body stamped with relics of her.

She moves her fingers to the space just below my elbow, to the basic wave inked into my skin. My brother has the same one—I know she remembers by the way she swallows, attempting to hold in the tears I know will fall anyway.

The soft touch has my eyes welling too, my chest constricting and my heart seizing.

There's no escaping this pain tonight, but we don't have to bear it alone.

I flip back the comforter, helping her crawl inside. I slip in beside her, bringing her head to my bare chest as her tears drip onto my skin. I cry with her, rubbing her back, kissing her head. We're quiet, outside my occasional reminders that she's not alone, that I'm here. They only make her weep harder.

I hold her until she falls asleep. I lie awake until the sky turns from black to blue to purple like the bruises across our souls, ensuring she gets the rest I know she needs. It's daylight when sleep finally claims me, Elena's heavy breathing like a lullaby.

She's my reprieve. My lifeline. My reminder there is light at the end of this tunnel.

For all that has been lost, for all the pain and all the guilt, for the conversations we haven't had yet, and the destruction they may cause, she's still here, still in my arms.

Nothing may ever be okay again, but we're still holding on to each other.

Chapter Twenty-Three

August

Three Months After Plus One Day

"my tears ricochet" - Taylor Swift

I wake hours later to an empty bed, a desolate house, and a hollowed heart.

Keep reading for a sneek peak of
Vice & Violet,
the conclusion of August and Elena's story.

Prologue

Violet

Four Years Ago

"hoax" - Taylor Swift

I was under the impression that March equaled the start of spring—blooming flowers, sunshine, the hope of a new dawn. Shit like that.

However, the frigid gust of wind that stings my cheeks as I climb out of the Fourth Street and Washington Square subway station feels like an omen of despair.

I use two fingers to zoom in on the map on my phone screen, figuring out which direction I need to take to find my dropped pin. I have to go three blocks north, then take a right down Tenth Street, and that should lead me right to her door. Though, I've gotten lost three times so far today, so I'm not overly hopeful.

I asked Monica for the address in passing, making it sound like I was going to send her a card of some sort. Thankfully, Monica didn't press for the occasion, because it's nowhere close to her birthday or any other card-worthy holiday we'd be celebrating.

That was three weeks ago. I quietly booked my flight out here and then told my friends—her family—that I was going to spend the weekend with my parents in Palm Springs. I knew nobody would ask questions about that, because my parents don't speak to them anymore. They don't speak to anyone, including me.

Somehow, I make my way to the address Monica provided me. It's a charming red-brick building with steps leading up to one entry, but numerous black fire escapes and white-framed windows looking out onto the street tell me they must all be apartments.

I walk up to the front door, finding a metal panel with unit numbers—each one paired with a circular button. I recheck my information, confirming that she's 313, and press the buzzer for her apartment.

It goes unanswered.

"Come on, Elena. You fucking coward," I growl, buzzing her again after a minute passes.

The wind picks up, and I wrap my coat tighter around myself. I definitely should've worn more layers. I didn't pack for an extended stay, because hotels in Manhattan are expensive as fuck, and I have no idea how this interaction might go with her. I wanted to prepare myself for pain—more than the pain she already caused me when I woke up that morning months ago—and somehow, it felt like if all I had was a carry-on when I ran back to California with my tail between my legs, it'd hurt less.

Despite expecting this to all go poorly, I couldn't not try. I gave her time and space. Six months' worth of it, really, but I know her better than anyone on earth knows her. She's been brewing and hiding and letting her emotions build. Eventually, the adrenaline and the shock are going to bottom out, and the grief and guilt will set in, if they haven't already.

Partially, I'm fucking angry at her for isolating herself from me. Another part of me is fucking terrified that she blames me, and that she'll never look me in the eye again without seeing him. Most of me, though, is just desperate to know exactly what's going on inside her head so I can fix it. I've always been able to see her in ways others can't. I've been able to read the words she can't express, and I think that's why she ran from me. She's not ready to address this, and she knows the moment she looks into my eyes, all that she's been suppressing is going to rise to the surface.

So, I'm angry with her, but more than anything, I fucking miss her. I've been destroyed without her, and I'm fearful of the guilt that comes alive when I look at her—the kind I felt that night when she was sleeping in my arms—but I'm not afraid enough to never see her face again.

I gave her three months to run and hide in New York, and now I'm cashing in. She's going to see me, she's going to talk to me, and she's going to hear me out. I'm going to fix this, fix us, because even after everything, I still believe we're meant to be.

Fate makes it hard to feel like it's on my side when I realize she isn't home right now, though.

I sigh, backtracking down the steps and taking a stroll around the block. I pick up a scarf, a sandwich, and a Coke from the bodega on the corner before I return to her building. I ring her buzzer three more times with no answer before I settle in on the bottom step and wait.

Either she's inside right now and ignoring me—in which case, I'll wait her out. Or she's not home, and that just means I'll be right here when she shows up. Even if I end up sitting here all night, New York is the city that never sleeps or whatever, so I don't need to either. All I know is that I didn't fly three thousand miles not to see her fucking face.

I put in my AirPods, bundling the scarf around my neck and chin, and tuck my hands inside my coat as the sun sinks low on the horizon, causing the temperature to drop further. Hozier blasts inside my ears, and nerves swirl in my bones, but I settle in to wait, feeling hopeful for the first time since that late night in January.

The sound of laughter startles me from the daze I must've dozed off into. My eyes fly open as I sit up straight, realizing I was leaning against the handrailing of the stairs. I check to ensure my backpack is still on the ground between my legs, thankful it didn't get swiped.

It's completely dark now, though the illumination of the city around me makes it feel damn near daylight. There are still dozens of people strolling along the sidewalks, dipping in and out of apartments, bars, and restaurants on the street in front of me. It's lively and cheerful. I can understand why people love New York so much, though I'm not sure I'd ever be able to justify living somewhere where I can't see the stars.

I wonder if that's why this is the place Elena ran to. I wonder if she's trying to avoid the sky I remind her of.

That laugh chimes again, closer this time. I know that laugh better than I know my own heartbeat. I can still remember the way it racked against my chest the first time I heard the sound when I was just a kid. The way I'd do anything to hear it over and over.

I stand up, swiveling my head down both sides of the street in search of that laugh, of her. I don't know how she's going to react when she sees me, but I hope it's enough to get me through her door and give me a chance to explain why I'm here.

I finally catch sight of her rounding the corner of a nearby alley. She's not paying attention to where she's going, arms linked between two people. A girl with short, platinum-blond hair and a blue beanie, and a tall, lanky man who gazes down at Elena like she hung the goddamn fucking moon.

She skips between them, dark curls bouncing, her beautiful face bright with carefree laughter.

What the fuck?

Two other people follow behind them, and the tall man

says something I can't decipher before the rest of them burst into laughter again. Elena lets go of the girl's arm, allowing the man next to her to twirl her in circles right there on the sidewalk. She giggles the entire time like a fucking schoolgirl before he tugs her into him, snaking his arm around her waist.

I feel sick.

I hop off the bottom step and duck behind the staircase that leads to her building, listening as she makes conversation with this group of strangers, her voice growing louder with each passing second. My mind reels and my stomach drops because she sounds clear. Happy, even.

For months, she shut herself away from not only me, but from her brothers, her parents—every fucking person who loves her. For months, she didn't eat, she didn't sleep, and wouldn't speak. She missed the goddamn funeral, for fuck's sake.

According to Everett, she claimed she was falling behind on deadlines, that she needed a fresh place to focus, and what better setting for a writer than New York City? I assumed she was using it as an excuse to rot in silence, because while Elena may be fine falling apart herself, she doesn't like to watch others worry for her. I assumed it was the mask she always wears, pretending she's okay when she's breaking inside. I assumed that she'd tumble into darkness on her own out here, and I've laid awake every night in the three months since I discovered she'd boarded that plane, wondering if she was okay.

I put my own grief on the back burner to prioritize hers. Stopped caring for my well-being because I needed her to be okay, and when she wouldn't let me fix her, I wrecked myself in solidarity, even if she wasn't there to witness it.

Because when she came back home, I wanted her to know that I waited to heal. Waited for her, because I've been determined to do it together.

But as I hide behind a brick wall in the middle of Manhattan, listening to the love of my life laugh with another man, I realize that I've been crumbling all on my own.

I bite my fist to quell my scream as I hear her unlock the main door to the building, the shuffle of multiple footsteps leading inside. Clearly, she's made a pretty new life for herself here in New York, out on a Thursday night with friends while I've been waiting for her in California, destroying myself in the process.

When our world burned down around us, I thought she was lost in the flames right beside me. Now that I'm standing in the ashes of the house we built together, I realize I've been alone the whole goddamn time.

To be continued...

Vice & Violet

AVAILABLE NOVEMBER 4, 2025

Acknowledgments

First and foremost, I want to thank every reader who has joined me here in Pacific Shores. Those who have fallen in love with this small town, this family, and these characters, who have been anxiously awaiting August and Elena's story for years now. Your endless support has made so many of my dreams come true, and I'll never be able to express my gratitude fully. Thank you for loving this series so loudly.

My husband, Bubs, for always reading the pages of my soul written in a language no one else understands. For knowing me better than anyone else, and loving me more for it. For the care you take and the assurance you relentlessly provide. You are the reason I write love stories.

My Jenna, because your role in my life goes beyond titles. You're more than a brand manager and more than a friend. This story would not exist without you. Thank you for every late night Facetime, brainstorm session, and for holding all of my sanity in your hands. I could not function without you, and I would not be living out my childhood dreams without your support.

My team, Cassie and Page, for keeping me on track and keeping my feet moving when I feel like I can't do it myself, and for loving my stories as much as I do. I couldn't do it without you!

Lexi, the literal other half of my soul. There are a lot of reasons I believe in soulmates, but you may be the number one. I'm objectively a better person, friend, and writer because I know you. Augustus is all for you.

My beta readers, Cait, Elle, Tori, and Maddy. Thank you for

helping me believe in this book during the moments when I felt so unsure, and for consistently supporting it, recommending it, and talking about it during this delay in publishing. Your support means everything to me!

My agent, Katie, for all your support in making my publishing dreams come true. I couldn't do it without you.

The Page & Vine Team for taking a chance on my little universe and bringing it to stores all over the world. You make me feel like the luckiest author alive.

The incredible indie bookstores and small businesses who have supported me and this series so loudly: Wildflower Fiction, Scribbles Bookshop, Heartbound Bookshop, Always Yours Bookshop, Love and Other Books, Pages of Passion, In Bloom Fiction, Jadestone Creates, and Well Read Candle Co.

My editors, Alexa and Jordyn, for taking this story and this series to new heights, and for always supporting my vision and my voice.

My street team. I love you, my horny little gremlins. Thank you for your endless love and excitement over these figments of my imagination. You keep me going most days, and I couldn't be more thankful for your support.

Author friends who I wouldn't make it through the day without, Bailey Hannah, Ambar Cordova, Cali Melle, and Emily Tudor. Thank you for being in the trenches with me.

August, Elena, & Zach's Playlist

Chapter One
"Jump Then Fall (Taylor's Version)" by Taylor Swift

Chapter Two
"Hey Girl" by Stephen Sanchez

Chapter Three
"Please Don't Be" by Hazlett

Chapter Four
"Video Games" by Lana Del Rey

Chapter Five
"august" by Taylor Swift

Chapter Six
"illicit affairs" by Taylor Swift

Chapter Seven
"Love Me Anyway" by Chappell Roan

Chapter Eight
"Guilty As Sin?" by Taylor Swift

Chapter Nine
"that girl" by Kenzie Cait

Chapter Ten
"Tolerate It" by Taylor Swift

Chapter Eleven
"the 1" by Taylor Swift

Chapter Twelve
"i'm worried it will always be you" by Katie Gregson-MacLeod

Chapter Thirteen
"History Of Man" by Maisie Peters

Chapter Fourteen
"Violets for Roses" by Lana Del Rey
"Ultraviolet" by Aiden Bissett

Chapter Fifteen
"Heavenly" by Cigarettes After Sex

Chapter Sixteen
"When The Night is Over" by Lord Huron

Chapter Seventeen
"The Black Dog" by Taylor Swift

Chapter Eighteen
"How Did It End?" by Taylor Swift

Chapter Nineteen
"epiphany" by Taylor Swift

Chapter Twenty
"Indigo (featuring Avery Anna)" by Sam Barber

Chapter Twenty-One
"Love Letter From The Sea To The Shore" by Delaney Bailey

Chapter Twenty - Two
"would've been you" by sombr

Chapter Twenty-Three
"my tears ricochet" by Taylor Swift

About the Author

Sarah fell in love with reading as a child. She quickly learned that books can take her to all the places she always dreamed of going, and allow her to live endless lifetimes in the one that she was given.

Sarah believes that to be seen is to be loved, and that's why romance is such an important genre. She believes romance novels offer readers reflection and relatability, ultimately helping us understand ourselves, and the world around us, a little better. She prides herself on crafting healing, raw, and uplifting stories that explore the complexities of the human spirit through the guise of love.

Sarah was born in California and raised in Southern Oregon, and still considers herself to be a Pacific Northwest gal at heart; right down to being a coffee snob, collecting hydro flasks, adamantly believing in Sasquatch, and never having owned an umbrella.

She now resides in Arizona with her husband and their pup, Rue. When she's not writing, she's reading, and if she's not reading, she's probably out searching for a decent cup of coffee or binging Vanderpump Rules for the millionth time.

Connect with Sarah on social media: @sarahabaileyauthor

Sign up for her newsletter to be the first to know about updates and announcements: sarahabaileyauthor.com/newsletter

Also by Sarah A. Bailey

Pacific Shores series
Heathen & Honeysuckle
Wicked & Wildflower
Reckless Roses
Vice & Violet

The Soulmate series
The Soulmate Theory
The Fate Philosophy
The Forever Experiment

Celestia Cove series
Coming 2026